Freya Harte is not a Puzzle

MÉABH COLLINS is a writer from Dublin. She holds an M.Phil in Children's Literature from Trinity College Dublin, where she is currently pursuing a PhD. In recent years, she has worked as a primary school teacher and in children's and Irish-language publishing. She lives in Dublin with her husband and their well-dressed rescue greyhound. This is her first novel.

Freya Harte is not a Puzzle

Méabh Collins

THE O'BRIEN PRESS
DUBLIN

First published in 2023 by
The O'Brien Press Ltd,
12 Terenure Road East, Rathgar,
Dublin 6, D06 HD27 Ireland.
Tel: +353 1 4923333; Fax: +353 1 4922777
E-mail: books@obrien.ie
Website: obrien.ie

The O'Brien Press is a member of Publishing Ireland
ISBN: 978-1-78849-345-1
Text © copyright Méabh Collins 2023
The moral rights of the author have been asserted
Copyright for typesetting, layout, editing, design
© The O'Brien Press Ltd

1 3 5 7 8 6 4 2
23 25 27 26 24

Cover design by Emma Byrne
Internal design by Emma Byrne

Printed and bound by Nørhaven A/S, Denmark.

Freya Harte Is Not A Puzzle receives financial assistance from The Arts Council

Published in

Do mo thuistí

Chapter 1

For the third time this month, I find myself sitting on the plastic chair outside Ms Connolly's office, my hands clasped between my knees, as I wait for her to call me inside. Her office door is slightly ajar, and I can hear the incoherent mumble of her voice on the phone, punctuated here and there by polite laughter. I try not to think about her, or my presence on this too-familiar brown chair that creaks every time I lean back. Instead, I focus my attention on the poster across the hall. 'Great Irish Writers' the title reads, and there are twelve sepia-tinted images of writers below. I count the number of glasses, moustaches and ties I see. They are all men.

The sound of footsteps approaches and Ms Connolly pokes her head into the corridor. 'Right then, Freya. Shall we?'

I follow her inside.

'You're supposed to be in Geography at the moment, correct?' Her eyes are fixed on her computer, where she has pulled up my timetable.

I nod.

'More trouble with Ms Kavanagh, I take it.'

It is not a question.

She sits back in her chair and looks at me, tilts her head to the side in that way adults do to let you know they're *really* listening. 'Why don't you tell me what happened this time.'

I shift awkwardly in my seat, sink my teeth into my bottom lip, pinning my mouth shut. I know that as soon as I try to speak my voice will wobble and a film of tears will coat my eyes. It's not that I've done anything wrong (I haven't), but being wrongfully accused of something in front of your entire class and being sent to the Vice-Principal's office as punishment is a humiliating experience that would surely make anyone want to cry.

But Ms Connolly is nice, I remind myself. She has been kind and understanding about everything this year.

I take a breath. 'We were looking at Ordnance Survey maps,' I begin, tugging at the scratchy sleeve of my school jumper (yet another thing I hate about secondary school). 'Ms Kavanagh asked me to find a tourist attraction on the map of Carrick-on-Shannon, and I pointed to the little blue symbol, which means boating activities.' I pause and look up at Ms Connolly, who is still sitting back, eyes fixed on me. I can't read her expression. I return my gaze to my lap and continue.

'Ms Kavanagh asked me which *specific* boating activities were there, and I said that it was impossible to know from just the symbol because it could mean water skiing or fishing or basically anything that happens in a boat. Then *she* said that I had to be more specific, because that's what the examiner would expect, and *I* said that wasn't true, you only had to say 'boating activities'. Then *she* said–

'How do you know that you don't have to be more specific?' Ms Connolly says, sitting forward now and knitting her fingers together on the desk. She looks... amused, I think.

'Because the map doesn't show you what's actually there, it only shows the symbol. And Ms Kavanagh said a few weeks ago that you only have to identify the *symbol*.'

'And now she's saying you need to be more specific.'

'Yes. Which you don't.'

Ms Connolly's brow creases. 'Freya, can you remember the reason Ms Kavanagh sent you to see me the last time?'

I have to stop myself from rolling my eyes. 'The thing about the food chain. She said that camels eat storks in the desert and that it's all part of the circle of life. I said that camels are herbivores and that that was impossible, and *she*,' – I stop myself from saying *went ballistic* – 'wasn't happy. She said I was *giving her lip* and sent me here. But I wasn't giving her anything,' I add defensively. 'I was just pointing out her mistake. It's not my fault that she makes so many.'

Ms Connolly nods her head thoughtfully. 'I wonder, Freya, if Ms Kavanagh thought you were trying to get a rise out of her when you did that. Do you know what I mean?'

I shake my head.

'Is it possible she thought you were being cheeky?'

My eyes are now rolling of their own accord.

'Now, look,' Ms Connolly continues, '*I* know that's not what happened. But Ms Kavanagh doesn't know you like I do. She hears a student challenging her or speaking up without raising a hand and thinks the worst. She thinks you're being belligerent, trying to make her look foolish.'

I chew the inside of my cheek as I consider this. 'But what am I supposed to do when Ms Kavanagh teaches us things that are wrong? What if desert climates come up in the Junior Cert and everyone writes about camels eating storks? Isn't it unfair on the rest of the class if I *don't* point out her mistakes?'

'Of course, but I'd like us to think about ways you can do that and also be,' – Ms Connolly searches for the word – '*mindful* of Ms Kavanagh's feelings.'

This is the part I hate. The part where, although we've established that I've done nothing wrong (on the contrary, I was being helpful), I'm in trouble for not being polite enough about it. 'Ms Kavanagh wasn't mindful of my feelings,' I mumble, wincing at the memory of the other girls sniggering as I was ordered out of the classroom. A tear slips onto my skirt.

'If she knew, she wouldn't be so hard on you,' Ms Connolly says softly. 'Maybe it would be a good idea if we tell her why these... *misunderstandings* keep happening. I know you said you'd rather keep things to yourself but, at the end of the day, teachers want the best for their students. They can only help you reach your full potential if they understand you properly.'

'But then everyone will know,' I say, wiping my wet cheeks with the heel of my palm.

'They won't. I promise you they won't. It's confidential information.'

'But I'll start getting special treatment and they'll know something's up.'

Ms Connolly lets out a clipped, exasperated laugh. 'Freya, I guarantee you every one of your classmates is too consumed by her own worries to even *think* about you. They won't notice a thing.'

I think Ms Connolly greatly underestimates the beady eyes of bored schoolgirls.

'Tell you what,' she continues, 'since it's only really Ms Kavanagh you've been having trouble with, we could just tell her. We don't need to tell your other teachers yet. Does that sound OK?'

I nod reluctantly. Part of me relishes the thought of Ms Kavanagh clumsily trying to defend herself when Ms Connolly confronts her. How guilty she'll feel when she realises how spectacularly unfair she's been.

'All right then. Look, the bell's about to ring for lunch. Why don't you head down to the library?'

I stand to take my leave.

'And Freya?' Ms Connolly calls as I press on the door handle. 'You know you have nothing to worry about, don't you? You're a wonderful girl and a wonderful student. A diagnosis doesn't change anything. It just helps us to understand you better.'

I push the toe of my shoe into the flecked grey carpet. 'Yes, Ms Connolly.'

If I don't show my face in the Third-Year common area, everyone will think something far more dramatic occurred in Ms Connolly's office and there'll be further gossiping. I steel myself as I walk past the lunch tables, try my best to ignore the heat in my cheeks and lick of sweat coating my spine. As I pull my lunchbox from my locker, Orla appears.

'So, what happened? Did you get detention?'

Typical. She has expressed precisely zero interest in keeping my company this year, but can always be relied upon to come sniffing for details whenever I get into trouble. I can just picture it: the whole class laughing after I was thrown out by Ms Kavanagh, keen to know what happened next, and Orla generously offering to approach the weird girl on their behalf. *It's OK*, she'll no doubt have assured them. *She thinks we're friends*. My jaw clenches and I shut my locker door more forcefully than intended.

'Of course I didn't,' I say, affecting a casual tone of voice and breezily brushing past her for added effect. 'Ms Connolly needed help checking the names of next year's First Years. Since I was already there, she asked me to do it.'

Orla looks disappointed. 'She didn't even write in your journal?'

I give my best exasperated sigh, which I hope conveys impatience at this tedious line of questioning. 'Why would she? Ms Connolly used to teach Geography. She knows all about Ordnance Survey Maps. She actually thanked me for bringing Ms Kavanagh's incompetence to her attention. She said Leslie Park was one of the best schools in Dublin and that there was a certain standard to uphold.'

I fidget with the clasp of my lunchbox as the lie falls from my lips, but Orla seems to have bought it. She smiles weakly to mask her disappointment. She will have nothing to offer her new friends, no morsel of entertainment from her encounter with the class freak.

'At least you're not in trouble,' she says vaguely, and drifts back to her table.

In the library, I spread the contents of my lunchbox across the empty desk: two satsumas (it doesn't count as a full portion of fruit if you only eat one), a tuna sandwich (toasted makes it easier to digest) and a cashew bar (a good source of iron when eaten with the oranges).

'Are you planning on eating any of that or just staring at it?' a voice says behind me.

I turn around and see Shannon Mulhern leaning over the back of a chair. I turn away again without responding.

'Here, are those cashew bars any good?' Shannon asks. 'My mum gets the ones in the blue wrapper. They're made from dates, I think. They're grand. Better than the cacao and orange ones, which just taste like regurgitated jaffa cakes.'

I have no idea what to do with this pile of ramblings and focus my attention on Ms Horgan's Wall of Inspiration instead. She prints out quotations from famous authors and mounts them on colourful cardboard speech bubbles every week. It's a lot of effort, but it makes this windowless old classroom feel more like a real library, while our new one is still being built. This week, a pink bubble reads: *Life, with its rules, its obligations, and its freedoms, is like a sonnet: You're given the form, but you have to write the sonnet yourself. – Madeline L'Engle.*

'Len-gle,' Shannon whispers.

I turn and look at her blankly.

She points to the bubble. 'It's pronounced Madeline *Len*-gle. In case you were going to get all French about it.'

I frown. Shannon is the one catch to being on the Third-Year Library Committee.

That evening, I lie tummy-down on my bed and sketch a picture of Scrump, the ugly doll from *Lilo and Stitch*, in my journal. As I add the stitching detail to its button eyes, my mind replays the events of the day. I'm frustrated with myself for having landed in yet more trouble with Ms Kavanagh and for how I handled my interaction with Orla. She'll never want to be my friend again if that's how I talk to her, and I'll continue to float through school like a weird, friendless ghost. I set my pencil down and look at my drawing. It's my best Scrump yet, I think. I've had a lot to think about this evening, a lot of fuzzy energy to push through my pencil.

I hear the front door open and scoot my journal under my bed before heading downstairs. In the kitchen, Mum fixes the kettle into its cradle. She has taken off her coat, but her bicycle helmet is still on her head.

'Hi, love,' she says cheerily. 'Had you a good day?'

'Fine,' I say, leaning against the counter and fidgeting with a bobbin on my wrist.

'Good. I'd a long day myself. I'm still up to my eyes with emails from the students about fees and registration.' She shakes her head. 'Anyway, did you eat today? Sorry, I meant have you had dinner? I was going to pop a few salmon fillets in the oven, boil up some broccoli and baby potatoes. Very healthy.'

'Sure,' I say indifferently, as if food hasn't been a tiptoe subject between us for the last few months.

Mum looks quietly relieved. 'So, how was school?'

'Fine,' I say, then quickly scramble to pad out my response. 'Except the teachers are all talking about the Mocks in January, which is still ages away.'

I'm not usually so forthcoming with details about the school day, but I need to distract Mum in case she catches on to the Ms Kavanagh incident.

The kettle starts to rumble on the counter. Mum reaches for an old Donald Duck mug and makes herself some tea. 'No harm in getting a head start on the study, I suppose,' she says. 'And how's Orla getting on? I haven't seen her in a while.'

I twist the hair bobbin around my fingers, cutting off circulation. 'She's fine.'

'Great. And how's Katie finding college?'

My fingers are throbbing from the pressure of the elastic. 'Likes it,' I say, as if I have any clue.

'That's good. God, can you believe it? Katie in college and you and Orla doing the Junior Cert. I don't know where the time goes. I can still picture the pair of you here, singing your hearts out for me and Dad at one of your sleepovers. What was that song from the Rapunzel film again? The duet you always sang together.'

'Can't remember,' I lie, and stretch the bobbin from my

thumb to my baby finger and around again. It snaps and goes flying across the room. I shake out my hand as the blood flow returns to my fingers. 'Can we make dinner now?'

'Of course. Sorry, love.'

She begins fumbling with the knobs on the oven and I'm suddenly consumed by giggles at the sight of her.

'Freya?' She looks up at me. 'What's so–'

I have to cover my mouth to stop myself from spluttering. 'Your helmet,' I say. 'You're still wearing it.'

'Oh,' she says, touching the side of her head self-consciously. 'What am I like? I knew I was forgetting something.'

I laugh again and let the sound burst into the air unchecked. I bask in the feeling of relief it brings. Home is the only place I can do this. The only place I feel safe enough to let everything out, whatever messy shape it takes. The only place I can be myself.

Chapter 2

I'm still reeling from the flustered look on Ms Kavanagh's face when she saw me in the corridor this morning. It was obvious Ms Connolly had spoken to her, and although part of me regrets that she now knows my weakness, an even bigger part of me is relieved. She can't single me out anymore, can't humiliate me in front of the others. I doubt she'll even speak to me again.

'Freya, are we listening?' My Irish teacher, Mr Regan, waves a hand in my direction. I hear murmurs of laughter around me as I compose myself.

'*Brón orm,*' I mumble.

Mr Regan raises an unimpressed eyebrow.

'Right. Now, as I was saying, we've the Oral coming up after Christmas, and anyone taking it is invited to do an intense prep course in the Slievanure Gaeltacht over Midterm. Ms Garvey teaches at a college there during the summer and has arranged everything for us.'

A hum of excited whispers fills the classroom.

'Will all the Irish classes be going?' a girl called Izzo asks.

'Any Third Year student who wants to can attend. You'll be taught by local teachers in the area, and myself and the other Irish teachers will supervise.'

'Where will we be staying?' Izzo's best friend, Chloe, asks, reaching excitedly for Izzo's hand across the desk.

'You'll be split into different houses around the village and a *bean an tí* will look after you. Just like on the summer courses.'

Then Orla raises her hand. 'Can we pick who we want to stay with?'

Her question gets the biggest reaction of all as it occurs to the others that they will have roommates. Chloe reaches across to squeeze her hand too, and Orla looks as deliriously excited as a dog with a bone.

Orla had worked hard on befriending Izzo and Chloe last year. They had been positioned as popular from the early days of First Year, so it wasn't hard to see why she coveted their friendship so desperately. She made all kinds of efforts to win them over, from changing her route to school to walk with them, to buying them lavish birthday presents and writing them notes in class exclaiming how much she loved their headbands. She probably would have won their affection sooner had I not been clinging to her the whole time, hurting her image.

'OK, settle down,' Mr Regan says as my classmates chatter excitedly. 'I take it you'll want to pick your own roommates then.'

19

A collective high-pitched squeal tears across the classroom. I flinch at the sound.

'Right. Decide among yourselves and I'll send around a list tomorrow.'

For the rest of class, little attention is paid to Mr Regan and his efforts to teach us the *modh coinníollach*. I watch as the others lean over their desks when his back is turned, whisper and fire scrunched up notes at each other across the classroom. All the while, butterfly wings beat frantically in my chest. I am not excited about picking roommates. I have nobody to choose and nobody will choose me. I burrow my fingertips under the hem of my skirt, dig my nails deep into the sides of my legs to control myself. *Don't cry,* I warned myself. *Not now. Not here.*

As soon as the bell rings, I rush out of the classroom, stash my books in my locker and grab my lunchbox. I wind through a sea of navy woollen jumpers until I reach the makeshift library, then quickly claim my usual spot at the edge of the cluster of desks. I have hardly steadied my breathing when Shannon walks in.

'You know, you're going to have to find somewhere else to eat your lunch when the new library is finished,' she says, eyeing my lunchbox disapprovingly and taking a seat in what I've grudgingly come to accept as *her* usual spot. 'There's no way Ms Horgan is going to allow food in her shiny new library.' She glances over at the school librarian, who is busy cataloguing boxes of books in the corner of the room.

'I know,' I say, pulling my lunchbox towards me defensively.

'And you're going to have to do something on the committee besides spending lunchtime here. I don't think you can count *Freya ate lunch in the library every day* as an OAL, you know?'

I feel my cheeks start to warm. I can't tell if Shannon is giving out to me or being sarcastic. It's not like I wanted to be on the Library Committee. It was Ms Connolly's idea. She said Ms Horgan was looking for more Third Years to join and that it would be good for me to be more involved in school. She also said I could eat my lunch here, since it was only an old classroom anyway.

'Maybe if we both come up with a few ideas for projects, we can sit down and talk about them. You are *not* allowed to suggest making the new library a lunch spot though,' Shannon says. She looks disapprovingly at my lunchbox again, but in a more theatrical manner this time, which suggests she might be joking. I don't touch it just in case.

I watch as Shannon rummages through her bag. The sight of so many loose, crumpled sheets of paper and dog-eared copy books makes me uneasy. She whips out a slender paperback and holds it up in front of her. *The Perks of Being a Wallflower*.

'Ever read it?' she asks.

I shake my head. I've never even heard of it.

'One of my favourites. The main character, Charlie, reads all of these classic books that his English teacher gives him, and I'm making a list of them to read. Did you know that *Peter Pan* was originally a book? I thought it was just a pervy old Disney film.'

My jaw tightens. This is the real reason I don't like Shannon Mulhern. Not only is she bossy and annoying, but she openly hates Disney. Her CBA in English last year was dedicated to it. She dressed up as the old hag from *Beauty and the Beast* and gave a talk called 'Sexism in Disney Movies: A Tale As Old As Time'. Ms Lee gave her a standing ovation. I ground my teeth the whole way through.

Despite myself, I can't help asking Shannon what she thinks is wrong with *Peter Pan*. I inspect my nails to appear indifferent as she begins to rant.

'Well, "What Made the Red Man Red?" for one thing.' She screws her face in disgust. '*So* racist. And then there's the treatment of basically every female character. The guys say stuff like, *a jealous female can be tricked into anything* and are constantly humiliating them. Peter Pan literally *spanks* Tinkerbell to get her to produce more fairy dust. How messed up is that?'

I feign a neutral expression and shrug. I don't want Shannon to know how distressing I find having Disney, my favourite thing in the world, ripped apart in front of me like this.

'So, yeah,' Shannon concludes, 'it'll be interesting to see

what the original book is like. Hopefully poor Tink catches a break.'

She turns away to read, and I sit staring at my lunchbox, still unsure whether I should open it or not.

'A holiday in Slievanure!' Mum exclaims, looking up from the TV. 'That sounds lovely, doesn't it?'

'We'll have classes every day,' I reply, confused. 'And they're making us go during Midterm, when we're supposed to be off from school.'

'But you'll go on lovely walks and fill up on healthy sea air. It'll be great. How do we sign you up? Do I need to write a cheque?'

I am suddenly hit with the same feeling of punched-gut panic I felt in Mr Regan's class. I don't want to go on this trip. I don't think I *can* go on this trip. Four whole days away from Mum and Dad, sleeping in a different bed and eating strange food. And then there's the roommate situation. I can't handle the humiliation of being the only person without one, or of being placed in a room of girls I'm not friends with and who don't want me there.

'Are you all right, love?' Mum asks, and I realise there are tears slipping down my cheeks.

'I don't think…'

I feel my throat begin to close.

'Oh, Freya,' Mum says softly, pulling me in towards her. 'You're a bit *overwhelmed*, are you, love?'

Overwhelmed. That was one of our new words. One of the dictionary's worth we acquired during the summer.

I nod as Mum soothes my back.

'Is it the thought of being away from home? Because you're well able for it, and you'll have your friends looking out for you. Orla will be going, won't she? Maybe we just need to visualise it a bit. Isn't that what Elaine said to do whenever there's a new plan?'

Mum took everything Elaine, the psychologist who assessed me last summer, told us as gospel. She had a way of normalising things, of making a diagnosis seem like something that simply needed to be *managed*.

'Tell you what,' Mum says, smoothing back tear-wet hair from my face. 'As soon as the school sends home more information about the trip, we'll look closely at everything so that we'll know what to expect. I'm sure that when you see the place you'll feel better about going. And Orla–'

'Orla's not my friend anymore,' I say, suddenly prickly and pulling away from her.

Mum looks confused. 'What do you mean? Did something happen?'

'She just doesn't like me anymore, OK?' I cross my arms

tightly, feel a wall building up inside me.

'But why wouldn't she… the two of you are best friends. If something happened, I'm sure–'

'Things are different now. She wants normal friends.' I stare at my feet, determined not to catch Mum's eye.

'Normal?' Mum laughs in that same exasperated way as Ms Connolly. 'Freya, what on earth does that mean?'

I ball my fists tightly under my arms. 'Friends who aren't autistic.'

Chapter 3

I cannot think about autism without thinking about last summer. In a way, I'm relieved that the problems I'd been having before then are no longer invisible, but I'm not sure that being identified as autistic is the outcome I wanted either. It all unravelled in June, after school finished for the summer and I was suddenly home all the time. Mum and Dad started to notice some of my behaviours more, especially around food. It's not like I stopped eating entirely; I was trying to be healthy. It gave me a sense of control over my life. Sometimes I wonder if I should have tried harder to be more secretive about my eating habits. Another part of me wonders if I wanted my parents to notice.

Mum started watching me more closely at the dinner table and noticing that the fridge was still full when she came home from work. It was easy to leave my lunch behind in school, but now I had nowhere to hide, no way to lie. It was also getting harder to come up with new excuses for refusing certain food. I could tell her patience with me was wearing thin, and when I collapsed on the kitchen floor one afternoon, she and Dad didn't hesitate in bringing me to the hospital. They said they didn't know what else to do. I begged them not to, swore things weren't that bad and that I'd do whatever they wanted, but they had already lost trust in me. I can still picture their faces in that moment, tired and sunken with worry.

What I mostly remember about the hospital is the horrible clash of smells and noises, all disinfectant and squeaky vinyl floors. People retched and groaned in the seats around us, and I sank my head into my lap to block it all out. Eventually, a nurse called my name, and I was brought into a small curtained room away from the waiting area.

'Freya?' the nurse said, indicating a padded table covered with a paper sheet for me to sit on. 'I'm Angel.'

The sound of my name on a stranger's lips made me suddenly aware of how real everything was, how frightening. Mum and Dad explained to Angel that it had been days since I'd last eaten a full meal and that I'd been avoidant and sneaky around food for weeks, months even. They made it sound like I was doing it to hurt them. All I'd wanted was a sense of control, and now things were more chaotic than ever.

Angel carried out a series of tests on me, which involved things like standing up and lying down repeatedly while a thick band attached to a machine tightened around my arm. She then disappeared with her clipboard and returned a few minutes later with a doctor, who explained that I had a low resting heart rate and low blood pressure. He said that he was concerned about me, and advised that I stay in the hospital until I was stronger. He explained to Mum and Dad that what patients like me really needed was psychological attention, but that they could help me get physically stronger as a start. 'Well,' he added, 'until we need the bed back.'

The sound distorted around me then, until all I could hear was the sound of my own ragged breathing. They were going to make me *stay* here.

Chapter 4

Through the window of the library door I see Shannon reading and bristle. I don't want her to give out to me again, so I decide to eat my lunch in the corridor instead. My lunchbox under my arm, I stare at her as I peel a satsuma. Even the back of her head annoys me. Why does she care so much about being on the Library Committee anyway? And, more importantly, *what* is her problem with Disney? I know that it's no longer cool to like Disney and that I have to keep my love of it a secret, but outgrowing something isn't the same as hating it like Shannon does.

I am stuffing an orange segment into my mouth when my lunchbox slips from under my arm and crashes to the floor. Shannon whips her head around and catches my eye through the window. She makes a confused gesture and beckons me inside.

'Why were you hovering outside the door?' she asks as I take my seat.

'I was just… the door was stuck.'

She is uninterested in the lie. 'Want to hear something

crazy?' she says, eyebrows raised, holding up a copy of *Peter Pan* in a protective library cover. Her eyes are wide with excitement. 'The fairies go to *orgies*! Can you believe it? This is supposed to be a *children's* book. No wonder the Disney film is so messed up when this is the source material!'

I nod as if I have the faintest idea what she is talking about.

On her desk, I see that Shannon is working through an Irish worksheet.

'I just couldn't face doing it for homework,' she explains. 'I'm so bad at Irish. Seriously, I don't know how I'm going to survive trying to speak it for four days on that trip.' She makes a pained expression. 'Are you going?'

'I think so,' I say vaguely, knowing Mum has already signed the cheque.

'Cool. Do you know who you're staying with?'

My whole body stiffens. Will I have to stay with Shannon? I need to think of a lie quickly. 'Probably Orla.'

I feel queasy as soon as I say it. Orla would be furious if she got stuck with me as a roommate.

'Are you OK, Freya? You look like you're going to be sick,' Shannon says.

I realise I'm cradling my arms over my stomach.

'Just hungry,' I say, and turn away to finish the rest of my lunch.

The classroom thrums with excitement as we wait for Mr Regan to arrive with the finalised list of roommates. The other girls are already talking about what they're going to pack and who's going to bring hair straighteners and hair dryers to share. Mr Regan eventually appears and everyone stares at him intently.

'*Go bhfóire Dia orainn!*' he says. 'I have it here, don't worry.' He sets his teaching materials on the desk and holds up the list. 'Right, so our class will be split between two houses, with three rooms in each. Eva, Joy, and Fatimah will be in one room,' – a shriek of delight rings out – 'Jana, Lily, and Niamh will be in another,' – a second shriek – 'and Chloe, Orla and Isabella will be in the last room. Oh, and Freya.'

Orla whips around in alarm. I catch her eye, but before I can gesture or mouth anything, she turns her back to me.

'Why did you put me on your list?' Orla asks me at my locker after class. 'We never said we were going to be roommates. You knew I was going to pick Izzo and Chloe. We wanted a three-person room.'

I press my fingers into the open door of my locker for support. 'I didn't put your name on my list. I didn't even have a list.'

It's true. Mr Regan had collected our lists the day after he announced the trip and I had deliberately arrived late to class so that he wouldn't ask for mine.

Orla rolls her eyes. 'You don't have to lie about it.'

'I'm not lying. I didn't write a list.'

'So, what? It's just a coincidence that he put us together?'

I'm not surprised by her anger, but I am hurt by it. Would sharing a room with me really be so terrible?

'Maybe he thought we were friends,' I offer, saddened by the reminder that this is clearly untrue.

'Whatever. Just... don't get in my way on this trip, OK?'

She doesn't hang around long enough for me to respond, not that I'd have any clue what to say anyway.

When Mum appears at my bedroom door after work, I feel suddenly frustrated about everything. 'Did you ask Mr Regan to put me with Orla on the trip?' I demand.

Mum is taken aback. 'I didn't say anything, Freya. Why? What's happened?'

'We're in the same room together, *obviously*.'

'Is that a bad thing? Orla's your...'

'She's not my friend! You know she's not my friend. Why do you keep acting like she is?' I'm not used to raising my voice like this. It hurts my throat.

'Freya, I didn't do or say anything to get you in the same room as Orla. I don't know anything about it. Should we try to have you moved? I'm sure Ms Connolly would be happy to help.'

'No,' I say, taking a cushion and hugging it close to my belly. 'Just leave it. Things are already ruined.'

'I'm sorry you're upset, pet,' Mum says. I think she's going to try to comfort me more, but instead she says, 'Your dinner is downstairs when you're ready.'

She shuts the door gently behind her, and I curl onto my side. Orla and I were further away than ever from being friends and it was all my fault. If I wasn't so terrible at secondary school – if I wasn't always so embarrassing – then maybe she wouldn't have been so eager to distance herself from me. Why was it that, no matter how hard I tried, I always managed to stand out in a million terrible ways at school? I was always forgetting things and arriving late to class, and teachers were constantly giving out to me for not paying attention and even being rude. I had no idea how to make new friends, and even when I tried copying the other girls, I still got it wrong.

Mum said secondary school was a big jump from primary and that it might take a while to feel settled there. I believed her at first, but if everyone was finding secondary school as hard as me, they were amazingly good at hiding it. Did everyone else bite down on their tongues to stop themselves from blurting out the wrong things at break time? Did they feel disoriented moving through crowded, too-loud corridors, or exhausted from changing classrooms so many times a day? I was now in my third year of secondary school and still nowhere close to getting it right.

Chapter 5

t surprised me how calm I felt inside my blue curtain on the hospital ward. After spending an afternoon hooked to a drip in a corridor, Mum and Dad either side of me like bodyguards, I was grateful for the privacy it provided. In a funny way, I felt safe there, all the stresses of the world temporarily removed. I was going to get better now, Mum promised. I'd had a stressful few months, but soon I'd be better, and wasn't that great news? Yes, I agreed. All I had to do was eat more while I was here, then she and Dad would help me to make a meal plan at home. Yes, yes, yes, I agreed. I did want to get better, but what Mum didn't understand was that wanting to get better was what put me here in the first place.

After two days, just like the doctor predicted, the hospital needed the bed back. By then, I'd been taken off the drip and was eating real food again. I held my breath and screwed my face at anything that wasn't one of my safe foods, but still I swallowed it all. I needed to prove that I was trying, that I could be trusted to get better.

I thought I'd spend the rest of the summer following the

new meal plan I'd negotiated with Mum and Dad (I'd agreed to add a few more foods to my safe list), but Mum had other ideas.

One night, I heard her and Dad talking in the kitchen. I was hovering on the stairs, listening, my sensitive ears picking up every word.

'She'll grow out of it,' Dad said. 'Teenage girls are always going on diets.'

'*Teenage girls* don't usually end up in hospital over it,' Mum said. Her voice was spiky and unfamiliar.

'Tom went through that phase with the protein shakes a few years back. This is probably similar to that,' Dad said. His pained efforts to sound reassuring made me cringe.

'Tom played football. He trained. This isn't the same at all. Freya's been skipping meals and restricting food for months. She's been lying and sneaking around us so that we wouldn't notice.'

It was hard to listen to them talk about me like this, like I had deceived them. It wasn't like that at all, but they never asked to hear my side of things. I wouldn't have had the words to explain myself anyway.

'We're going to meet with a lovely lady called Fiona next week,' Mum announced chirpily the next day. She and Dad were seated at the kitchen table when I entered the room. I stared at them blankly.

Mum, stirring her tea a little too vigorously, continued: 'I'd a long chat with her this morning and she's certain she'll be able to help. She's a therapist and says she sees this kind of thing a lot in girls your age.'

This kind of thing. Mum was trying to minimise the situation. Maybe this was her way of feeling in control.

To everyone's relief, it turned out I liked Fiona and didn't mind meeting with her. She spoke in a soft Donegal accent and didn't make me feel strange. We worked through worksheets together in our first few sessions, which I found much easier than talking about my feelings. Feelings, for me, were hard to pin down. They fluttered around me constantly, but I often struggled to catch and name them. Filling in worksheets was much more straightforward. I couldn't always see the relevance of them, like when they focused on the deceptiveness of photo editing and advertising, but it was nice to pretend that my problems stemmed solely from the pressures of social media. It made me feel normal.

Fiona began to probe me more about school, my interests, my friendships. She wanted to learn about the things I found difficult in secondary school, like making new friends and being organised. She seemed very interested when I told her that I thought school was like an ice rink, and I was the only person there without skates.

One day, after our session had ended, Fiona asked to talk to Mum. I waited in the corridor outside her office, but heard every word. 'I might be wrong,' she said, 'but sometimes symptoms of eating disorders and autism overlap. I see a lot of girls Freya's age who struggle with disordered eating; sometimes their behaviour is a symptom of something else that's been missed. It might be worth considering an assessment.'

'They're just trying to put her in a box, Tríona,' Dad said that evening. They were in the kitchen, while I lingered on the stairs. I was getting used to eavesdropping on conversations about myself. Getting used to feeling like a ghost. 'Whatever she goes in for, they're bound to find something to label her with. It's how they do things nowadays,' Dad said. He was using his reassuring voice again. 'But she's just Freya. We'd have figured it out by now if there was something more going on.'

'But see on this page, this thing about auditory processing,' Mum said, dismissing his comment. I could picture the blue light of the laptop screen drowning her worried face. 'Remember the hearing tests we brought her in for when she was little, when we thought she was slow to respond to us. Her teachers still say she doesn't listen half the time, but maybe there's more to it than that. And look here, where it mentions sensory sensitivities. She's always been so easily irritated by noise and touch and smell. Remember all the tantrums about itchy fabrics and wrong foods? We were always quick to call her sensitive…' Mum trailed off. 'Her mood is different, Colm. It has been for a while. She's so… inside herself. The not-eating is only the tip of the iceberg. She's struggling with something deeper, I can sense it.

'It's called being a teenager,' Dad replied. 'We all have to go through it.'

Mum ignored him. 'I'm going to call the clinic Fiona mentioned. I think we should have her assessed.'

Chapter 6

'm making my way to Ms Connolly's office at the end of the day, wondering why she has asked me to see her. Had I forgotten something? Misplaced something? Was I in trouble with another teacher? I don't think I was late to any of my classes today.

'Thanks for dropping in, Freya,' she says as I shut the office door behind me. 'Take a seat. I wanted to check in about the Midterm trip, see how you're feeling. I had a word with Mr Regan about making sure you were with a friend. You had mentioned Orla before so I thought...'

I feel my skin contract. Ms Connolly is responsible.

'Anyway, the other classes have submitted their lists, and your name popped up on one of them.' She checks the sheet of paper in front of her. 'Shannon Mulhern. She's on the Library Committee too, isn't she? If you'd like to stay with her instead that would be no problem at all. We could move you into another house.'

'No,' I say quickly. 'I want to stay where I am. With Orla.'

'Right,' Ms Connolly says. 'I just wanted to be sure. How

have you been otherwise, Freya?'

I squeeze my fingers into my palms and look down at my feet. 'Fine.'

'Everything OK with your teachers?'

'Mm.'

'You know you can always drop in here if there's anything you'd like to chat about.'

'OK.'

'I was thinking, after Midterm we could start looking at study skills together, maybe have a weekly session. It might be useful with exams coming up. What do you think?'

'OK.'

She opens her mouth to speak, then pauses, as if caught on a thought. 'You know, I was thinking recently about an old student of mine who was diagnosed with dyslexia when she was in Sixth Year. She'd never been a brilliant reader, but nobody thought it was a serious problem either. Her teachers just thought she was the disorganised type, to be honest, a bit of a daydreamer. Turns out she'd spent years memorising books and avoiding reading aloud. She was also quite the talker and a bit of a comic. Looking back, I think she was trying to distract from her challenges. Nobody likes to make mistakes, but I think girls often want to seem perfect at all costs.'

'Or normal,' I reply absently.

Ms Connolly smiles. 'I hope we can do more to help you

in school now, Freya. I was looking through some of your old reports the other day, and I was struck by how often you run out of time and misinterpret questions in exams. A lot of teachers have said that you don't listen in class either. I think your diagnosis explains a lot of these things. So much of it is about processing, isn't it? Needing to do things at a different pace or in a different way in order to succeed. What do you think?'

I tug at my sleeve reflexively. 'Yeah,' I say, not looking at Ms Connolly because I don't know what the right answer to her question is. I don't want special treatment in school. I don't want to be singled out for being different. If I could just figure out how to be normal, then I wouldn't have to worry about this stuff.

It occurs to me on my walk home that staying in a room with Orla is an opportunity for us to become friends again. I had been worried about her being mad at me for the whole trip, but really I should be focusing on how to use the situation to my advantage. If I plan carefully enough, I might even win over Izzo and Chloe in the process. The thought of having almost lost this chance because of Shannon makes me clutch it all the more tightly.

At home, I pull out my sketchpad from under the bed and flick past my many doodles of Disney characters to an empty page.

Things I will be in Irish college:

1. Friendly to everyone (and agree with everything they say)
2. Easy-going (let the others pick the beds/ use the shower first etc.)
3. Nice (compliment everyone's clothes/shoes/make-up etc.)

Things I will not be:

1. Annoying (don't ask too many questions)
2. Slow (don't drift out of conversation and lose track of what's going on)
3. Weird (no stupid comments)
4. Embarrassing for Orla (don't bring up primary school stuff or Disney)
5. _AUTISTIC_

Chapter 7

On Fiona's advice, Mum and Dad arranged for me to meet with a psychologist called Elaine. They had already talked to her and given her detailed forms about me, which included school reports going all the way back to Junior Infants. After that, everyone agreed that I should meet Elaine in person. The clinic she worked in was outside Dublin, and I made a Disney playlist especially for the car trip. It felt a bit like going on holidays, except instead of arriving at a rented cottage by the sea, we arrived at a third-floor office with hard leather seats and a box of children's toys in the corner.

Elaine gave me time to settle into our meeting, then gradually eased into her many questions. To my relief, she didn't start with food.

'Tell me about Orla,' Elaine said. 'She's your friend from primary school, isn't she?' I nodded and shook my head simultaneously, resulting in a confusing gesture.

'She's not your friend?' Elaine said, trying to interpret.

When I didn't reply, she continued guessing.

'Perhaps things have changed between you?'

I nodded.

'Well, would you like to talk about what happened?' Her question caught me off guard and my hands started to feel twitchy. Elaine offered me a stress ball to play with and told me to take my time.

'She doesn't like me anymore,' I said, pushing the words out as quickly as I could. 'She wants new friends.'

'Why do you think that is?' Elaine asked calmly. I squeezed the ball as hard as I could to stop myself from crying.

When I felt composed again, I told Elaine about how Orla had begun physically blocking me at lunchtime by turning her back to me in the common area and stretching her arm across the table as if I wasn't there. I told her about the time in First Year when Orla kicked my shin after I started singing the *Tangled* duet to her, and how she changed her route to school to walk with Izzo and Chloe, even though it was quicker to pass by my house.

'And what were things like when you were in primary school?' Elaine asked.

'We were best friends,' I said, which I presumed explained everything.

'And what did you do as best friends?'

I shrugged. 'Went to each other's houses, dressed up, watched films.'

For every example I gave of things Orla and I did together,

Elaine wanted to know how we organised ourselves and made decisions. I told her that, when we sang Disney duets together, Orla was always the female lead, and when we reenacted scenes from our favourite films, she always got to pick her character first.

'It sounds like Orla was in charge a lot. Would I be right in saying that?' Elaine asked.

I tossed the ball between my hands. 'Mm.'

'Did you mind that?'

'Not really.'

'And what would happen if you and Orla disagreed on something?'

I squeezed the ball and watched as it slowly returned to shape in my palm. 'Sometimes she called me stupid.'

'That's quite an unpleasant thing to hear. Would she say that often?'

I shrugged. Orla often got annoyed with me when I got things wrong or got over-excited when we were playing. Sometimes I sat too close to her, or was too loud or hyper. Sometimes she'd ask what I'd eventually learn were trick questions, like if I thought her spots were bad or if she needed braces. I was always honest with her, but it turns out flattery was what she was looking for. It wasn't until I observed her with Chloe and Izzo that I finally figured this out.

What are you talking about, you're so pretty!

No way, your hair is stunning like that!

Honestly, I can't even see what spot you're talking about!

Complimenting each other excessively and lying to make each other feel better was how you made and kept friends in secondary school, I learned, but by then it was too late.

'When you were closest, what was your favourite thing about Orla?' Elaine asked.

'That she was my best friend,' I said simply. What more was there to say?

I was surprised to learn that Mum and Dad had spent most of their meeting with Elaine talking about when I was a baby. They told her that I hated being held by anyone other than Mum, while my brother, Tom, loved being picked up or played with by anyone. Apparently, my sense of smell was so strong that Mum had to leave the house while she was weaning me off breastfeeding. If I knew she was nearby, I'd cry and refuse the formula Dad was trying to feed me. They also told Elaine about disagreements with other children at playschool and how I wasn't always good at sharing or taking turns. They told her I was often happiest in my own company, making up games in the garden or drawing in my room. I wondered how Elaine could make meaning from all of this seemingly random information about me, but that's exactly what she did.

When Elaine finally explained to us that I was autistic, there was no drum-roll moment or tense opening of an envelope. She simply handed Mum and Dad a copy of the report she'd written and went through it with us in her office. She also gave me a booklet called *Autistic and Proud!*

'Autism was often viewed as a negative thing in the past,' she explained, 'but that's starting to change. Autistic people are reclaiming the narrative. This is a booklet of some really brilliant autistic people doing great things in the world, even teenagers as young as you.'

I took the booklet from her, even though it felt irrelevant to me. I had enjoyed my meeting with Elaine, but I wasn't sure I agreed with her assessment of me. She'd caught me at a bad time, but that didn't mean I was autistic.

Chapter 8

I'm waiting at the LUAS stop when I spot Orla approaching the small green on the opposite side of the tracks. It's Saturday and I don't recognise the clothes she's wearing, although it's been a while since I've seen Orla in anything other than our school uniform. I'm relieved that my outfit – my non-school uniform, as I think of it – matches hers. We're both wearing black leggings, block colour hoodies and white runners. The only difference is I have my school bag with me, which is not something I can explain if she spots me. I can't risk her seeing me and asking what I'm doing here. Not when my plan for Irish College is to convince her I'm normal.

I watch as she takes a seat on the steel bench and curse myself for having slept in. I usually make this trip much earlier in the day, when most people – or at least Orla and anyone else from school – are still asleep. Orla's eyes are fixed firmly on her phone, her thumbs busy typing. I presume she's messaging Izzo and Chloe. I presume they're going to Dundrum. Would other people be there, too? Boys from one of the other schools? Does Orla have a boyfriend?

I hide behind the platform shelter so that she doesn't see me. What if Izzo and Chloe are on their way to meet her? What if they ask where I'm going on a Saturday with my school bag? The ticket tagging machine is at the other end of the platform though. If I go over, there's a chance Orla will notice me. *Think, Freya.* I've made this trip every fortnight for the last few months and never once encountered an inspector. I have a decision to make: stay where I am and sneak onto the tram without tagging my Leap card, or go over to the machine and risk Orla spotting me.

The LUAS arrives and grinds to an abrupt halt at the platform. The doors open and I scurry on board without another thought. I face away from Orla and feel lighter as the tram starts moving. I've made it unnoticed. I take a seat and set my empty school bag on my lap. Only three more stops to go.

As we reach the next platform, my breath catches. A group of inspectors in navy jackets and orange high-vis vests is waiting for our tram to pull in. They form a line as we stop, ready to catch anyone who might try to evade them.

The doors slide open and they saunter in casually, setting up their handheld ticket scanners and adjusting their lanyards. Blood pulses inside my ears as they move through the carriages. I watch as they interact with the other passengers, take their tickets while laughing jovially and remarking on the weather. My chest is thumping now, my back sweating. Why didn't I tag my card? Why did Orla have to be there at the exact moment I was supposed to do it?

'Ticket please, miss,' a man with greying hair and a ginger moustache says.

I pointlessly retrieve my Leap card from the front pocket of my school bag and hand it to him.

'Looks like you didn't tag on, sweetheart,' he says through a mouthful of chewing gum.

A prickling sensation creeps up my limbs and reaches my neck, my scalp. It feels like tiny little needles are pressing everywhere into my skin.

'Oh,' I say clumsily. 'I thought…' I trail off, unable to commit to the pathetic lie.

The inspector stops chewing. 'I'm going to have to ask you to step out with me at the next stop, sweetheart.'

My neck is too stiff to nod.

The tram stops and I follow him out, my cheeks burning as the eyes of my fellow passengers press into me. I clutch my school bag to my stomach for support.

'What's your name, sweetheart?' the inspector asks, pulling a small notebook from his back pocket.

I open my mouth to speak, but the words dissolve on my tongue. Instead I stand there with my eyes closed, as if trying to make myself disappear.

The inspector huffs. 'Do you think I was born yesterday,

sweetheart?'

Stop calling me sweetheart. Stop calling me sweetheart.

I shake my head vigorously, feel the pressure building behind my eyes. *Hold it in*, I will myself.

'You're not the first young one to pull this kind of thing, you know.'

But I don't know! I don't know anything except that my breath is short, my hands are clammy and I am struggling against my instinct to cry right now.

'Oh, for the love of… look, just tag your card and get on the next tram. We can forget about a fine this time, OK?'

I nod my head desperately, manage to release some kind of sound from my throat.

He smirks, shakes his head. 'You young ones. Nothing but trouble.'

I press my Leap card against the tagging machine until it pings, then wait next to an elderly woman with a wheeled shopping carrier for the next tram. The inspector swings his lanyard around his finger nearby and sings a song about a girl called Sharona. I try my best to ignore him. When the next tram pulls in, I rush towards it and pretend not to see him waving with his fingers in the reflection of the glass doors.

I find an empty seat and melt into it as we take off. This tram is fuller than the last, but that doesn't stop me exhaling dramatically in front of my fellow passengers. I must look deranged as

I press my hands over my eyes and try to steady my breathing. Nobody seems to notice, or at least they pretend not to. I'm so close now. I just need to keep it together a bit longer.

I reach my stop and walk quickly towards the newsagents, avoiding the eyes and accidental touch of strangers as I go. When I get there, I head straight past the ice-cream freezer in the middle of the floor to the magazine rack at the back wall. I scan the various glossy covers until I find it. My Disney magazine. The thing I came all this way for. My heart swells at the sight of it and I bring a copy to the till immediately. The sooner I can get home to my room and put this morning behind me, the better.

'Isn't this a lovely magazine?' the woman behind the counter says, scanning the barcode. She holds it up to take a closer look. 'Fifty dolls to collect! You'll be bankrupt!'

I laugh awkwardly, then take the magazine from her to stash in my bag.

The woman tells me to have a nice day and I smile vaguely in return without meeting her eye. I need to get home. This trip was never usually this stressful, but it was always inconvenient. Getting the LUAS to another suburb every other week to buy a limited-edition Disney magazine with a porcelain doll was tiring work. I could have bought it from a shop closer to home, but I risked getting caught by someone from school that way. As far as I'm aware, most fourteen-year-olds don't spend their pocket money on children's magazines.

At home, I race up the stairs and shut my bedroom door behind me. I draw the curtains, curl onto my bed and let the weight of my stress crash over me at last. I can cry now. I can let it all out. *You are safe,* I tell myself over and over again. *You are safe, you are safe.*

In moments like this, I feel like Snow White after the Huntsman has told her to run away from the castle. In her panic, her surroundings warp and her beloved forest becomes a frightening place, all snares and shadows. She becomes tangled in powerful vines and gets attacked by clawing branches. Her animal friends turn on her, startling her with their squawks and cries, while a ferocious wind chases after her. She becomes dizzy, increasingly confused in her surroundings until she can't help but scream and throw herself into a heap on the forest floor. The frantic music fades as she lies there, her whole body shuddering as she cries. Then it's over. The shadows disappear and the animals are no longer threatening. The sun breaks through the forest. She begins to feel OK again.

Elaine described this experience as a 'meltdown', but to me they've always been Snow White Moments. They were scary when they happened – my body and mind crashing simultaneously like an overheated computer. They weren't always easy to control either, but I was getting better at squashing them down until I was alone.

When I feel calm again, I pull my school bag onto the bed and take out my magazine. This week's doll is Aladdin. I remove him from his packaging and run my fingers along his glossy black hair and clothes. He is cold to touch, his porcelain limbs stiff and unpleasantly creaky. I reach under my bed and pull out the large box from Mum's winter boots. This is where I store the other dolls (Aladdin is the tenth in my collection) with their respective magazines. The magazines are childish and not particularly informative, but I keep them as part of my collection anyway.

I lay the dolls on the floor and admire them, adjust their clothes and dust their features with my fingertips until they are perfect. I feel peaceful when I do this, like nothing else exists around me. It's what I need on days like today, when the world has twisted itself into a frightening forest. It's what helps me come back to myself. *You are safe now, Freya. You are safe.*

Chapter 9

'Didn't I give you pocket money a week ago?' Mum says, transferring a mound of wet clothes from the washing machine to the laundry basket.

'I spent it,' I say sheepishly, hovering over her. I don't want to tell her what I've spent it on. She'd only scoff at the price of the magazines and tell me I was wasting my money.

'How much?' she asks irritably, pulling loose socks from inside the feet of a pair of tights.

'I was thinking I could have an advance,' I say, unwilling to disclose the exact amount. 'Please? It's for the trip.'

Her face softens. 'Of course. We'll have to get you a few bits for it.'

'Just some new shampoo,' I say, 'and maybe some face wash. I want to bring some stuff for the room. To share with the others.'

The thought occurred to me as I was mulling over my plan to make Orla like me again. Orla loves sweets, and winning her back with bags of Haribo and Minstrels seems just as likely to work as anything else.

'That's a great idea,' Mum says encouragingly. 'And don't

worry about spending your pocket money. We'll go shopping together and get you what you need.'

By the time we reach Tesco, I've already figured out what I need to buy. A cursory glance at a few Zoe Turner videos on YouTube and I am more confident than ever about the trip. Zoe Turner is an influencer everyone in my year is obsessed with, and she's just launched a collection of beauty products in supermarkets.

'Eight euro is a bit expensive for a face mask, isn't it?' Mum says when I bring her a selection of products. 'How many did you say you'll need?'

'Four. One for each of us.'

'Ah, Freya. That's too much. Here, these ones are less than half the price. They'll do, won't they?'

'They need to be the Zoe Turner ones,' I insist.

Mum ignores me and wanders away from the beauty aisle. 'Let's have a look to see what else is here. We can always come back this way.'

'Please, Mum,' I say, stalking after her. 'You said we could buy whatever I needed.'

'I thought you meant a few bags of sweets or something. I'm not spending over €30 on a few scented rags with some pop star's face on them.'

'*Influencer*,' I correct her.

'It's too much, Freya. Why don't you pick up a few bags of Haribo instead? You always loved the Star Mix.'

I am tempted to remind her that I haven't eaten Haribo or any other kind of refined sugar product in almost a year, but restrain myself. 'Please, Mum. All I want is the Zoe Turner face masks. We don't have to get shampoo or any of the other stuff.'

'Freya, I've already told you no. I'm sorry, but we just can't be splurging on these kinds of things at the moment.'

She doesn't say it aloud, but I know what she's suggesting. I don't say another word.

'So, who are the other girls you'll be staying with?' Mum asks on the drive home, as I stare vacantly out the window. 'I know Orla, of course, but what about the others? Chloe and... Izzo, is it? That's an unusual name.'

'It's short for Isabella,' I mumble.

'Are they nice girls? I suppose they must be, if you've made friends with them.'

'I haven't made friends with them.'

'But you know them a little bit, don't you? You're all in the same class, aren't you?'

Her ignorance is astounding. 'I don't know them,' I say firmly.

'Well, you'll get to know each other on the trip, I suppose.'

'No, I won't,' I snap. 'I won't make friends with them on this trip or ever in my life because of you.'

'Freya, that's not fair,' Mum says, glancing at me disapprovingly before returning her gaze to the road.

'You're the one who said we could buy whatever I needed today and then you changed your mind. They're not going to want to spend time with me now and it's all your fault.'

'I didn't think you were looking to spend so much money.'

'That's why I asked you for an advance on my pocket money!'

'It's too much, Freya. I already told you that.'

I cross my arms. 'Well, then I'm sorry I made us poor.'

'Poor? We're not… why would you think that we're—'

'Because you and Dad had to spend all of our money on that stupid clinic last summer.'

Mum pulls in outside the house and takes a breath. 'It's just been a lot at once. And don't forget Tom's in Manchester now. We have rent and university fees to pay for him, too.'

'Why did you send me to Elaine?' I say, looking at my scowling reflection in the wing mirror.

'Because we wanted to do everything we could for you. And everything we discussed with Elaine made sense. All the problems you'd been having at school, with food…'

'I wasn't having problems,' I argue. 'Just because I'm not good at school, it doesn't mean there's something wrong with me. And just because I stopped eating *some* foods, it doesn't mean I was starving myself. Everything was fine before I went to see

Fiona and Elaine.'

'But Freya, everything wasn't fine,' Mum says. 'I don't think any of us truly understood that until now. There were always things your dad and I wondered about, but we never realised how much you'd been holding inside. You were barely coping, and then you weren't coping at all.'

I rest my head against the window. 'I'll never have friends again.'

'Darling, you will,' Mum says, taking my hand in hers. 'You went through a lot this summer, between the hospital and sessions with Fiona, to meeting Elaine. I know it's been a lot to take in, but I really think this diagnosis is a good thing. It's like a little guidebook, you know? It helps you – helps *us* – to understand how you see and feel things. It's nothing to be ashamed of.'

That was what Ms Connolly said too. But of course it was something to be ashamed of. Who wanted to be autistic? I'd like to have believed it was just an endearing quirk, like mismatched eyes or a gap-tooth smile. But it wasn't. To be autistic was to be so far from normal you needed a special word for it. That was why I couldn't accept it, why I refused to let Mum and Dad tell anyone but Ms Connolly. The adults in my life might have been convinced my diagnosis was correct, but I could still prove them wrong.

Chapter 10

'Tom says he'll be home for Midterm,' Mum says in the kitchen, as she fixes me a cup of peppermint tea. 'Or, half-term as they call it there.'

'Great,' I say absently.

'It'll be good to see him again, won't it? Hear all his news.'

'Mm.'

I tried to act like I missed Tom, but I was secretly relieved when he moved to Manchester for college in August. His habit of taking my food from the fridge and ignoring my many labels was particularly stressful last year. I'd come down for breakfast to find the blueberry punnet ransacked or half a bag of walnuts pilfered. Mum and Dad told him not to take food with my name on it, but he never listened. He said the kitchen was a communal space and that, unless I was paying for the food myself, it belonged to the whole family.

'We haven't told him anything, by the way,' Mum says, catching my eye as she sets my tea down. 'It's your decision, what you tell people.'

'You can tell him if you want,' I say, dragging the tea bag

around my mug by its string. 'He'll just say I'm looking for attention anyway.'

Mum frowns. 'I'm sure he wouldn't.'

'He's not exactly my biggest fan.'

'He's your brother! He loves you, even if he doesn't always show it.'

I wrap my fingers around my mug and pull it close to me. I'm not convinced.

In my room, I feel a sudden urge to look at the *Autistic and Proud!* booklet on my shelf. I haven't touched it since the day I came back from meeting Elaine, but now part of me wants to add up all the ways it doesn't relate to me. Leafing through it, I'm surprised to discover that Elaine is the author and that she's compiled a list of young Irish autistic people to feature in it, along with famous people like Greta Thunberg and a woman who came second in *Britain's Got Talent* a few years ago. They're all aged between sixteen and twenty-one and Elaine has inter-viewed each of them. There's Rosie, fifteen, from Offaly, who loves animals and hopes to become a vet someday. A picture of her with her pet iguana, Iggy, crawling up her face deters me from reading anything more about her. There's also Macdara, seventeen, from Tyrone, who loves *Breaking Bad* and hanging out with his girlfriend, Clare. Then there's Rossa, sixteen, from

Galway. He's a beekeeper and writes a blog about it. In his picture, he's handling a wooden frame covered in bees and wearing a full beekeeper suit, complete with a veiled hat. Apparently, he has over twelve thousand followers on Instagram. I open my phone to take a look.

Rossa's Instagram feels a bit like stepping outdoors, with every photograph steeped in nature: birds flying overhead, wildflowers swaying in the breeze and plenty of bee content. In the middle of the nature-filled grid, one picture grabs my attention. It's an image of Winnie the Pooh dressed as a bee and swimming through a sea of honey. I recognise it from the song *Everything Is Honey* and tap into it. Rossa's caption reads:

Hands up if you love Winnie the Pooh! This was one of my favourite songs from childhood. It reminds me of visiting my grandad's hives in the summers and helping him bottle jars of honey. Although honey is delicious and I can understand Pooh's obsession, I don't like to eat it now for ethical reasons. Read my latest blog on responsible honey harvesting and why we need to be mindful of animal exploitation as well as cruelty. Link in bio!

I continue scrolling and another image catches my eye. This one is of a rainbow-coloured infinity symbol, which I recognise from the cover of Elaine's booklet. I tap the image, which is framed by cartoon bees, to see what Rossa has written about it.

Happy Neurodiversity Celebration Week everyone! As many of my followers know, I am proudly autistic and love being part of a vibrant and diverse community. Being autistic is such a central part of my identity and is the reason I think, feel, and express myself as I do. It is the reason I am such a passionate advocate for bees and an ethical beekeeper. I love paying close attention to the movement of the bees in my hives and learning new facts about them. When the world feels chaotic and overwhelming, I find it calming to read about honeybees. For example, I love the order of the honeybee hive and how every bee has a special role within it. I also love how honeybees have their own special way of communicating with each other. When the scout bees that patrol the hive find a good source of nectar or pollen, they share this information with forager bees through something called the 'waggle dance.' This is a movement that takes the shape of the number eight and tells the foragers the distance and direction of the source so that they can find it. As I was tracing my little sister Emma's finger over an illustration of the waggle dance recently, it occurred to me that it also looks a bit like the neurodiversity symbol. This got me very excited. Not only do honeybees work in a very orderly way, as many autistic people do, but they communicate in their own way too, just like autistic people. I think it's very fitting that the waggle dance resembles the neurodiversity symbol, and

it is just one more reason why I adore honeybees!

My eyes trace the illustration of the waggle dance and I see what Rossa means. I scroll back to the top of Rossa's page and tap the link for his blog. I must spend a while reading through his posts, because when I eventually look up from my phone, it's dark outside.

Chapter 11

Mr Regan has grouped us according to our rooms and asked us to write down five phrases we think will be helpful while living together in Slievanure.

'How do you say *I'm boooored* in Irish?' Izzo says, leaning over the back of her chair.

The four of us are seated around Chloe's desk. This is the most amount of time I've spent with them since Orla started ignoring me at the lunch tables last year.

'*Tá mé...* bored?' Chloe suggests. Izzo laughs dryly.

'OK, seriously though, we need to think of something,' Orla says. She taps her pen against a blank page in her copybook. 'What about, *turn off the light.*'

Izzo rolls her eyes. 'How do you say *Orla fancies Mr Regan?*'

Chloe collapses over the desk in giggles and I force myself to smile along even though I don't think the joke is funny.

Orla blushes. I can tell she is keen to start the task. If it were just the two of us, we'd have finished it by now.

'Apparently, they're letting us keep our phones in Slievanure,' Chloe says.

'Thank God. I honestly wouldn't go if they made us turn them in,' Izzo says.

'Yeah, it's not like real Irish College,' Chloe says.

'That's also why it's going to be so boring. There won't be anyone else there besides our year, and all we're going to do is learn Irish. The whole point of Irish College is dressing up and meeting guys,' Izzo says.

'Maybe the *bean an tí* will have a son,' Orla offers.

'Oh my God, the poor guy if she does. Izzo will eat him alive,' Chloe says.

'Not a chance,' Izzo says disgustedly. 'He'll be some farmer in weird jeans.' My eyes flit from one to the other as I try to keep up with them. I'm aware that this makes me seem quiet, or like I'm not paying attention, but my brain is working hard. It's scanning every word like an item at a supermarket check-out, *beep, beep, beep.* Trying to think of what to add to a conversation at the same time I'm processing it is more multitasking than I can handle.

They continue not doing the assignment, so I give my brain a break and start writing down some phrases. At least this way I'm being useful.

'I see there's a bit of messing there in the back,' Mr Regan says disapprovingly, looking at our table. 'Would Isabella's group like to share some of their ideas with us?'

Izzo snatches my copybook from my hands.

'We want to know how to say…' – she scans my list and practically dissolves into laughter as she reads it – '… *I like your pyjamas.*'

Chloe snorts. 'Oh my God, *Freya!*'

'That's a great phrase,' Mr Regan says. He writes it on the board and thankfully turns his attention to another group.

I try to focus on the rest of the lesson, but Chloe and Izzo are now whispering to each other in Irish that they like each other's pyjamas, erupting into giggles every time one of them says it. When some of the other girls look over, they feign embarrassment and pretend to compose themselves before breaking into hysterics all over again. Orla tries to include herself, but I suspect she finds this as tedious as I do.

The bell rings and we gather our things.

'Oh, Freya,' Izzo says, brushing past me. 'You are honestly too funny. I can't wait to see what you come up with on the trip.'

I smile crookedly and feel myself blushing. What did *too funny* mean? I suspect she's laughing at me, but maybe that was better than nothing. Orla doesn't look at me as she leaves the classroom. I can tell from the tightness of her jaw that she's not happy. I assume it's my fault.

At home, I take four Disney dolls from the box under my bed

and assign them new identities. Snow White becomes Orla, Pocahontas and Ariel become Izzo and Chloe and I become Cinderella. I stand the dolls in a circle, as if they're in conversation, and turn Cinderella to face Ariel.

Chloe, that colour is stunning on you. Where did you get your top?

Then I turn Cinderella to face Snow White and Pocahontas. *Here, take the whole bag. Honestly, I'm not even hungry. I literally ate so much on the bus.*

It wasn't hard for me to mimic the voices of my peers. I spent so much time eavesdropping on them in school and watching their conversations happen in front of me that I could easily impersonate their speech and voice inflection. In theory, I knew how to behave so that I never stood out among them. I knew what clothes to wear, how to style my hair, who to follow online. In theory, I knew how to be normal. It was in practice that I failed.

I smooth out Cinderella's gown and the suede fringing on Pocahontas' tunic and continue practising. I found it helpful to script conversations in advance of them actually happening, like I'm rehearsing lines for a play. Conversations were hard enough with their fast pace and unpredictable twists and turns, and I was already so focused on other things: trying to appear engaged and nod my head at the right moments, monitoring my body language, making sure that, when I spoke, my voice sounded animated. It was a lot to manage in real-time, but practising helped.

'I've been thinking,' Mum says at my door before bed. 'We should buy you some food of your own for the trip. In case what the *bean an tí* serves doesn't suit you. I don't want you worrying about it, not when you've been doing so well with your plan.'

Mum sounds formal, like she's given the idea a lot of thought. She's trying to be practical, but still she seems uneasy. Mum keeps a close eye on me these days, but food is still not something we talk about directly.

'What kind of food?' I ask as neutrally as possible, fingers and toes wiggling under the duvet.

'Things that you like. I don't want you getting upset if the food there isn't right. I think we should be realistic.'

'OK.' I smile to reassure her. I had thought about food on the trip, the kinds of meals we'd be served. Of course I had. It hadn't occurred to me that I could bring my own supply though, and the idea is reassuring. 'I think some of the other girls are bringing their own food, too,' I say, remembering a conversation I overheard in Irish class. 'A few of them are vegetarian, and one girl's coeliac.' I hope this makes Mum feel better. I'm surprised when she blinks tears from her eyes.

'Sorry,' she says, self-conscious. 'It's your first time away from home. I just want you to be safe and happy.'

'I will be. I'll be with Orla, remember?'

Mum sniffs and takes a seat at the edge of my bed. 'Course you will. It's been a lot this year, hasn't it?'

'What has?'

'Everything, really. It was such a busy summer and you were back to school before we'd a chance to get our heads around any of it. You've had a lot on your plate, Freya. Dad and I do realise that. And you've been so good about everything – meeting with Ms Connolly, sticking with your food plan. We don't tell you enough how proud we are of you, love, but we really are.'

People were often telling me how much I was 'dealing with' these days. Mum and Dad said that I had *a lot on my plate*. And Elaine said the same in our meeting, after I'd explained all of the things I found hard about secondary school.

I was busy pressing my thumbs into the stress ball and quite talkative in my distraction. 'We only had one teacher and one classroom in primary school,' I told Elaine without thinking. 'We knew where we were going every morning and didn't have to move after that. In secondary school, we have to move classes every forty minutes. It's like musical chairs and I always forget where I'm supposed to go next. The teachers are scarier too. They shout a lot and some of them won't even let you go to the bathroom during class.'

I was reminded then of the time this caused me to wet myself in First Year, but couldn't bring myself to tell Elaine about it. Mr Ryan was strict about not letting students use the bathroom during class time, but I had forgotten to go beforehand. It was the last class of the day, and I raced home as soon as the bell rang, but didn't quite make it in time.

'The bell was different in primary school, too,' I continued. 'It was like a xylophone and went *bing bong bing*. The bell in secondary school is more like an alarm. It always makes me jump. And I hate the hand dryers in the bathroom. They sound like they're screaming and they're so weak you have to keep your hands under them for ages. They hurt my ears.'

Elaine nodded. 'Is there anything else that bothers you about school?'

'My uniform. The sleeves make my wrists itch and my knee socks are always falling down.' A memory resurfaced then of an incident with Ms Kavanagh, who told me to pull my socks up when I arrived late to class one day and then gave out to me for being cheeky when I did. 'I hate having a locker, too. I always forget my keys and then I get in trouble for not having my books or my homework.'

'Do you get in trouble a lot in school?'

'I feel like I'm always in trouble with someone, somewhere. For being late, for not having the right books, for forgetting my homework, for saying the wrong things, for not listening.'

'It sounds like you have a lot on your plate in school,' Elaine said. I stared at the ball in my hands, my fingers aching now from squeezing it so long. I didn't have a lot on my plate, I thought; I was balancing plates – in my hands, on my head, on my feet. They were bound to come crashing down eventually.

'I only have four years left,' I said.

'Is that how you think of it? How many years you have left?'

I squeezed the ball once more with all my might. 'Pretty much.'

Chapter 12

Mum brings my bag downstairs and hugs me tightly in the hall. 'Have a fantastic time, love. Text me whenever you want to. Or call. I'll be here if you need anything. You're sure you have everything?'

'Yes,' I say, squeezing her back. Dad takes my bag and puts it into the boot, while Mum stands at the front door and waves us off.

'You'll be doing a local history walk on the trip,' Dad says in the car. 'The schedule said you'd be shown around by a man called P.J. Browne. Interesting guy. He's written a lot about fairy forts in the area.'

Dad wasn't typically one for small talk, but anything about local history always sparked his interest.

'Cool,' I say, half listening. I don't care about a history walk. I am too busy thinking about the next four days. It makes me feel jittery inside, like there's a shaken-up snow globe in my belly. I squeeze my fingers and toes tightly to settle it.

'Have a good trip, Freya,' Dad says in the carpark, leaning in for a slightly awkward hug. 'See you in a few days. Tom'll be here when you get home, remember. You'll get a few days with him before he heads back again.'

I watch him walk back to the car, then carry my bag towards the bus. Most of the other girls have already arrived and there's a buzz of excitement in the air as they peep inside each other's suitcases and make promises about swapping clothes. I scan their outfits and am relieved to see that I'm dressed the same as most of them, that the strict uniform of black leggings, white runners and block colour hoodies hasn't changed. Some girls are bolder in their style, wearing tie-dye T-shirts and baggy jeans. Good for them, I think, but it's safer to align with the majority.

I look around the group for Orla, but she isn't here yet. Izzo and Chloe are part of a wider group, but I don't go over to them. On a low wall at the edge of the car park I spot Shannon on her phone, wearing lilac cords, flowery boots and a Christmas jumper, of all things. Instinct pulls me towards her, but then I remember my plan. I have to save my energy for Orla, Izzo and Chloe. For making them like me.

A navy car pulls up and I feel my heart squeeze. I watch as Orla gets out and disappears behind the boot. Her mum, Angela, steps out and scans the crowd. She spots me almost immediately.

'Freya!' She waves me over. 'It's a long time since I last saw you. How are you, darling?' Her voice is as loud and theatrical as ever.

'Fine, thanks,' I say on cue.

The car boot slams shut and Orla reappears with her suitcase. Her expression drops when she sees me.

'Orla, I was just saying how long it's been since I last saw Freya. Isn't she looking well? I always knew you'd be gorgeous when you grew up, Freya. Didn't I always say that, Orla?'

Orla pretends to adjust the handle on her suitcase.

'Ah, Orla. You're here,' Mr Regan says, jogging our way with a clipboard. 'That's everyone then. I'm organising you all into pairs so we don't lose anyone when we stop for lunch. Will I put you both together?'

'Oh, absolutely,' Angela says, wrapping her arms around both of us and pulling us in towards her. The stench of her perfume makes the inside of my nose fizz. 'Sure, there's no separating this pair. Thick as thieves since day one, isn't that right?'

Orla wriggles free. 'I'm going to put my bag on the bus.'

She storms ahead and I follow Mr Regan.

'Bye, girls!' Angela calls. 'Have a ball!'

Orla doesn't sit beside me until the luggage compartment is fully loaded, the driver has taken his seat and Mr Regan has instructed us to put our seatbelts on. Then, she wastes no time in taking out her AirPods and turning to face the window. I hadn't imagined we'd talk much on the bus, but I figured she'd at least acknowledge my existence. I take out my headphones and open a new Disney playlist. When the duet from *Tangled* comes on, I nudge her gently and show her the screen, in the hope that it might spark her memory. She smiles tightly and returns to face the window.

Be normal, I remind myself. *Don't be annoying. Don't be embarrassing. Don't bring up stuff from primary school.*

At the front of the bus, I spot the top of Shannon's head. She is sitting alone.

I am a few playlists deep by the time we stop for lunch, and Orla practically runs off the bus to catch up with Izzo and Chloe. I decide not to follow them, to give Orla space until we get there. Hopefully she'll appreciate the gesture.

'Hey,' Shannon says sheepishly, stepping in line with me at the lunch fridge, where I'm inspecting the ingredients of the readymade sandwiches.

'Hi,' I reply. It's strange seeing her outside of the library.

'So, are you excited?' she asks.

'Yeah.'

'Me too.'

Neither of us sounds excited in the least.

A girl called Joy appears beside us. 'Hey, roomie!' she says, nudging Shannon and taking a can of Coke from the fridge next to us.

Shannon beams. 'Hey!'

I'm confused. Joy's in *my* Irish class, not Shannon's. How are they roommates when we were all assigned to houses according to our classes? They wander off to the check-out together and I'm left alone again.

Back on the bus, Orla continues ignoring me. I make her job easier by ignoring her back. At one point, she falls asleep and her head lolls onto my shoulder. I don't move. She wakes and pulls away dramatically, looking at me as if I've violated her somehow. This is already starting to feel like a long four days.

After driving through a series of winding roads, the bus pulls into the community centre at Slievanure and we are ushered into a draughty hall by a team of adults in matching blue hoodies. I feel woozy from the bus, but try not to let it show. Everybody else seems fine.

'*Dia daoibh agus fáilte!*' a woman with a blonde topknot says enthusiastically. 'Can everyone hear me?'

The group mumbles in response.

'My name is Nóirín and I'll be one of your teachers for the next few days. I run the summer colleges here with Dervla, your wonderful teacher.' She gestures to Ms Garvey, who blushes and waves timidly. 'I hope you're all excited for a few days of *craic agus comhrá* with us!'

Mr Regan starts clapping, but nobody follows suit.

Nóirín goes over a few rules, then calls out the names for each house. The hall fills with the thunderous sound of suitcases rolling along the floor, and I try not to wince too visibly. I stand near, but not directly beside Orla, Izzo and Chloe as we wait for our next instructions.

'OK, everyone staying in Tigh Jackie, come with me,' a man calls, and directs us towards a minibus outside.

'That's us!' Izzo says, leading the way.

We hand the driver our cases and pile into the van.

Another flurry of snow whips up inside me as we take off. I press my fingernails into the sides of my legs to steady myself. This was it. My chance to prove myself normal.

Chapter 13

'How do you say *hideous* in Irish?' Izzo says, her top lip curled in disgust as she takes in her surroundings. Wallpaper of pink and purple circles that look like bubbles covers the room and makes it feel like we're inside a psychedelic fish tank. On the window sill, crystal bowls of dried flowers emit an overpowering scent that catches in the back of my throat.

'So tacky,' Orla says.

'I think it's kind of cute,' Chloe says.

Izzo claims a top bunk for herself, while Orla takes the bottom and Chloe takes the single bed next to them. I take the second single bed on the other side of the room.

'It smells like rotten eggs in the hall. I bet we'll get food poisoning on our first night,' Izzo complains.

'This bed is so hard and uncomfortable,' Orla says, pressing her hands into her mattress. 'It's going to wreck my back.'

They take turns criticising everything about the house, and I copy Chloe by unpacking my suitcase instead of weighing in, in case I complain about the wrong things. I hadn't prepared for this topic and don't trust myself to improvise. I'm glad to be in the single bed at the edge of the room. We haven't been here five minutes and it is already beginning to feel crowded. I try to ignore the swirling feeling in my tummy.

'Oh wow, are you veggie, too?' Chloe says excitedly, gesturing to the bag of fruit and veg next to my suitcase.

'Yeah,' I say tentatively. This was a far more straightforward lie than food allergies. 'But I eat fish. My mum makes me,' I add, just in case I get caught out.

'My mum checked and apparently the *bean an tí* is going to give us a special option at dinner, but I still brought my own stuff too. Just in case she serves us toast or something. Can you imagine?' I could imagine, but I don't think that's what Chloe meant by her question. I begin sorting the contents of my food bag.

'We can't eat those,' Chloe says, pointing to the bags of Haribo I brought. 'They have gelatin.'

'Oh, I know. I brought these for the room. Sorry, I didn't know you were veggie, too.'

'Ugh, amazing,' Izzo groans, sliding down from her bunk to see what I've brought. 'Orla, you like these ones, don't you?' she says, throwing a bag of Tangfastics at her.

Orla catches. 'Thanks,' she says quietly, not meeting my eye.

'I brought a bag of the vegan Percy Pigs,' Chloe says. 'We can share them, Freya.'

I smile awkwardly. I don't know how I'll get out of eating

sugary sweets if they're being offered to me directly.

The colour scheme in the dining room is aquamarine, right down to the place mats. I appreciate Jackie's enthusiasm for bright interiors, but her taste is starting to give me a headache. There is a big table and two smaller ones in the room. The girls from the other two rooms are already seated when we arrive, and Izzo, Orla and Chloe sit at one of the small tables. There is no room for me to join them, and I try my best to appear unfazed by this as I take a seat at the big table instead.

'*Anois, a chailíní*,' our *bean an tí*, Jackie says, pressing her backside into the door and presenting the first plates of food. 'A light supper to keep ye going.'

She sets the plates in front of Orla, Chloe, and Izzo, then leaves to fetch more. I glance over to see what's being served. Slices of wafer-thin ham are rolled into flimsy logs next to a dollop of creamy coleslaw, a boiled egg, a slice of cheese, and a small bread roll. My stomach contracts at the sight of it all, and I'm grateful to have some of my own food with me.

Izzo pushes the plate away from her in disgust. 'The smell of that egg literally makes me want to puke.'

'The ham is practically see-through.' Orla says, holding up a piece with her fork.

'I obviously can't eat it,' Chloe says, pushing her ham with her knife onto Orla's plate. 'More for you.'

'Hey, I don't want your second-hand ham,' Orla says.

'Well it can't stay on my plate. I find it offensive.'

'Dare you to hide it somewhere, Orla,' Izzo says, a mischievous glint in her eye.

The girls at the other tables have started listening in at this point, their conversations quieting and heads discreetly turning.

'What? I'm not hiding it,' Orla says, clearly annoyed by the suggestion, but forcing a small laugh to sound easy-going.

'Oh, come on. Don't be such a wuss. Hide it…' Izzo scans the room for a suitable location. 'Behind that photo!' She points to a framed wedding picture on the wall.

Orla's cheeks brighten and she looks down at her plate. 'Izzo, come on. I'm obviously *not* going to do that.' She gives another small laugh to mask her discomfort, weaker this time.

'Oh, come on, Orla. *Please*! It'll be *so* funny!'

Orla shifts awkwardly in her seat. '*Fine*,' she says eventually, as if it's actually no big deal. She wants her new friends to think she is fun and good-humoured, up for a laugh. The whole room is watching now as she lifts the frame from the wall. I can't believe she is actually doing this.

The door swings open and Jackie's backside reappears.

'Right, who's next?' she says, turning and entering with more plates.

Orla starts. '*Tá an pictiúr go deas*,' she says, clumsily fixing the frame to the wall again.

Jackie laughs. 'Wasn't I gorgeous?' she says, setting down the plates. 'The little waist on me. I wouldn't have much luck fitting into that dress now.' She disappears again to fetch the last of the plates, seemingly oblivious to what she's just walked in on.

Orla takes her seat again. Her cheeks are bright red, the tendons of her neck jutting out like cables. She doesn't look at any of us, but rips apart her bread roll, shoves a large piece of it into her mouth and chews furiously. I remember these moods, how on edge they'd put me. Usually Orla would tell me what I did or said that was wrong, but she can't do that here. She has to be on her best behaviour with Izzo in the same way I have to be on my best behaviour with her on this trip.

'It was just a joke,' Izzo says half-heartedly.

Orla pretends to laugh, her cheeks fat with bread.

The room is quiet – uncomfortably so – and I'm relieved when the other girls resume chatting among themselves.

When Jackie arrives with the final plate, she realises that there is no one left to take it and does a quick head count. 'Who's missing?'

'Shannon,' Joy says. 'She's napping.'

Jackie huffs. 'Not without her tea, she's not. I won't be having complaints of hungry children under this roof.' Jackie sets the plate down beside me and goes to fetch Shannon. 'And I'll be making sure everyone's eaten enough before ye head off to bed,' she adds. It feels like a threat.

Shannon enters a few minutes later, ruddy-cheeked and blinking. She flops down beside me, the only seat left in the room.

'Kind of random to be wearing a Christmas jumper in October, isn't it?' Izzo says, watching her. She is keen to stir trouble this evening.

Shannon ignores her and begins buttering her bread roll.

Izzo is not satisfied. 'Do you not know how a calendar works? *Christmas* happens in a month called *December*, but in *October* we celebrate something called *Halloween*.'

I have no idea where she's going with this, but I'm glad I'm not sitting at the same table as her. The air around her feels more crackly than usual.

'I'm aware how the calendar works,' Shannon says. 'Thanks for your concern though.'

Izzo laughs. 'Not really sure why you're wearing a jumper with a reindeer on it then. Unless, oh my God… is this the only jumper you own?' She brings a hand to her mouth as if this is a shocking revelation.

'Get lost,' Shannon says.

Izzo straightens, a small smirk tugging at her lips. This is exactly the reaction she is looking for. 'Wow, touchy! Is someone on the rag?'

'Can you just leave me alone, please?'

Izzo rolls her eyes. 'Relax. I'm just buzzing with you. Why are you even here? You're not in our Irish class. I'm pretty sure you're in the *lower* class.'

I watch Shannon to see how she'll respond and my jaw drops as she picks up a slice of ham and flings it at Izzo's face. The whole room falls silent; the sound of ham falling onto Izzo's plate with a soft thud makes me cringe. I've never seen lunch meat weaponised like this and it makes me extremely uncomfortable. Not another word is spoken at Izzo's table for the rest of the meal, and the other girls lower their voices as they speak among themselves. Jackie returns to inspect our plates, and I eat more than I want to to please her. The thought of so many different ingredients clashing in my tummy makes me uncomfortable, and I wring my hands under the table to distract myself from thinking too much about it. I am so far from home tonight. So far from feeling safe.

Chapter 14

The next morning, Chloe and Orla make strained efforts at small talk to distract from the awkwardness of the fact that Izzo is still not speaking. 'I wonder what our teacher will be like,' Chloe says, as she brushes her hair on her bed.

'Hopefully sound,' Orla says, 'and not like Mr Regan. His eyes literally bulge out of his head when you pronounce your "ch" wrong.'

I've been watching them for the last few minutes, willing myself to add some bland comment or other to the conversation. Izzo's not the only one who hasn't yet spoken today. *Put a penny in the slot*, I encourage myself. *See what happens.* Then: 'Do you think our teachers have to share rooms like we do?'

Chloe and Orla look at me at once and it feels like that split second standing in front of automatic doors, when you're suddenly unsure if they'll open for you.

'Oh my God, hilarious,' Chloe says then, to my relief. 'Can you imagine Mr Regan and Ms Garvey in a room together?'

'Sharing bunk beds!' Orla adds.

'Mr Regan would love that. I bet he's told all his loser friends that he's on a romantic holiday with his girlfriend this week.'

We all look up upon hearing the signature snark of her voice. The first words she's spoken since last night. Chloe and Orla laugh a little too eagerly, clearly pleased to have their leader back. They wait for Izzo to get dressed and then all make their way towards the dining room. They don't even acknowledge me as they leave. I'd put them back together, but they don't seem to have noticed.

The three sit around the same table as yesterday and chat away like nothing happened. I'm certain that Orla is deliberately taking up more room than she needs to and that a fourth chair could easily fit, but I'm not going to make that point. *Be easy-going, agree with Orla about everything.* Shannon waves me over to the other table, where she and her roommates are sitting.

'Hey,' Joy says, scooting over to make more room for me on the bench. 'How'd you sleep?'

'Fine.' I'm hardly going to tell her about my mini Snow White Moment in the bathroom, how my too-hard pillow and scratchy bed sheets sent me over the edge in the middle of the night.

'Are you in a bunk?' Fatimah asks.

'I have my own bed,' I reply.

'Lucky. I am so not used to sleeping that close to the ceiling.'

'I'm not used to anyone sleeping above me,' Shannon says.

'It's unnerving. Eva is literally suspended by rusty springs over my head. I could easily be crushed to death by her.'

'No promises,' Eva says, proudly jiggling her belly.

Jackie enters the room and everyone quickly returns to speaking Irish.

'All eating up, *tá súil agam*,' she says, scanning our plates as she sets down another plate of toast. She leaves again and I unspool slightly.

'OK, her obsession with us eating is insane. She really needs to chill,' Fatimah says.

'Maybe she's an environmentalist and hates food waste,' Eva offers. 'I can respect that.'

'Then why is she serving us so much toast? A person can only eat so much toast, Eva!'

'What's up with the T-shirt, Shannon,' Joy says, pointing a butter knife at Shannon's chest.

Shannon is wearing an oversized pink T-shirt that says *It Costs A Lot Of Money To Look This Cheap!*

'Dolly Parton!' Shannon exclaims. 'My queen.'

'She's, like, a country singer, right?' Eva says.

'Well, yeah, but she's so much more than that,' Shannon says. 'Like, she sends free books to children all around the world, gives scholarships to people to go to college, advocates for LGBTQ rights. Plus, her songs are amazing. You have to listen.'

Eva shrugs. 'OK, I trust you. You were right about The Cranberries.'

'So, we made a playlist for our room yesterday,' Joy explains to me, 'and everyone added their own songs. We ended up with a pretty eclectic mix in the end.'

'Yeah, jumping from Dermot Kennedy to "Singin' in the Rain" is a whole vibe,' Eva adds, glancing coyly at Fatimah.

Fatimah shrugs. 'I stand by my choices.'

'I can't believe I left off Dolly,' Shannon says. 'I'm adding her now.' She takes out her phone and it prompts me to look at mine.

A message from Mum: **Morning love, hope u are having a nice time. Love you. Mum xxx**

Me: **Having a great time! Love you too xx**

It's not exactly the truth, but I do feel better being away from my roommates for the moment.

The bus arrives to bring us to the community centre, where we'll have our classes. Orla, Chloe and Izzo have claimed the three-seater at the back of the bus, so I stay near Shannon and her roommates and pretend not to notice.

'I can't believe we have classes in the morning *and* afternoon,' Fatimah says.

'I know. My Dad is fully expecting me to be fluent by the

end of this,' Eva says.

'At least you guys are actually good at Irish,' Shannon says. 'I mean, you have to be, if you're in Mr Regan's class.'

Eva scrunches her nose. 'I guess we're good by Leslie Park standards. I don't think that's saying much though.'

'Irish isn't actually as hard as everyone thinks,' Joy says. 'People complain about it more than they actually try to learn it. It's actually pretty straightforward as a language.'

Fatimah rolls her eyes. 'Ms *Gaelscoil* over here, giving us another lecture.'

'Yeah, spare a thought for us helpless monoglots, Joy. Not everyone casually speaks four languages,' Eva says, playfully flicking Joy's temple. The intimacy of the gesture surprises me. I could never do that to someone.

'Sorry, *four* languages?' Shannon says.

Joy sighs. 'Igbo, French, Irish, English.'

'She's just here for the free toast,' Fatimah says, and everyone laughs again.

In the community centre, we are divided up and sent to different rooms to meet our teachers. My classroom is bright white and sparse, with only chairs and a waste basket in it. A strip light across the ceiling emits a harsh, fluorescent glow, and the lack of furniture or a carpet means there is nothing to absorb sound. I suppress the urge to cover both my eyes and ears as we take our seats.

A woman with wavy red hair enters, sporting the same *Coláiste Spraoi* hoodie the teachers all wore yesterday.

'*Maidin mhaith, a chailíní,*' she says brightly. '*Is mise Michelle.*'

She writes her name on the board and asks us to greet her. We all mumble awkwardly on cue.

'So, today we're going to start with some basic conversation, just to get the juices flowing. Let's say two old friends have bumped into each other in the street. What sort of things might they say to each other?'

Michelle taps her whiteboard marker against her palm, waiting for someone to speak up. When nobody does, she points to Fatimah and motions her to the top of the class. Fatimah groans quietly and goes to stand beside her. The two begin interacting, with Fatimah regularly apologising for her pronunciation.

'There's no need to apologise, girls,' Michelle tells the group repeatedly. 'The Oral is about confidence. Confidence comes with good preparation. OK, let's go again.'

Fatimah returns to her seat and Michelle scans the room for a second role-play candidate. We all squirm under her watchful eye.

'You,' she says, pointing at me. 'Up you come.' My body stiffens. 'What's your name?'

'*Freya is ainm dom*,' I say slowly and self-consciously.

'OK, Freya, let's say we've just met for the first time and are getting to know each other. We'll have a normal chat about where we're from and what we like. OK?'

Michelle proceeds to ask me how old I am, where I'm from and what I like to do on the weekend. I feel less self-conscious knowing that my clumsy responses are as much to do with my mediocre Irish as my poor conversational skills.

'These are all excellent responses, Freya,' Michelle assures me. 'I wonder if you could ask me some questions in return though, just for this exercise. We'll go back and forth, like we're playing conversation tennis.'

We start again. With every response I give, I imagine hitting a tennis ball, and ask Michelle a question in return. I'm surprised by how much more fluid the conversation sounds.

'You see?' Michelle says. 'The more you think of it as a normal chat, the more at ease you'll feel with the examiner. You won't have to ask them questions in the exam, of course, but just thinking of it as a conversation, rather than an exam or an interview, can really help you mentally.'

I take my seat again and Michelle moves on to the next part of the lesson. I take down notes like everyone else, but really I'm thinking about conversation as a game of tennis, a ball that sails back and forth between two people. *Pock... pock. Pock... pock.* It seems obvious, and yet I've never thought about it this way. Maybe conversation isn't the elusive art form I thought it was, but a formula. I like formulas. They can be learned.

Chapter 15

We're lying on our beds, passively scrolling through our phones before dinner when Shannon peeks her head in the door.

'Can I talk to you, Izzo?' she says quietly.

Izzo looks up from her phone briefly before returning to scroll. 'Fine. Talk.'

Shannon fidgets with the door handle. 'I just wanted to say sorry about yesterday. What I did was really messed up.'

We all look up at Izzo. 'Cool,' she says, not lifting her eyes from her phone. 'You can go now.'

Shannon lingers for a moment before leaving, then gently shuts the door behind her.

Izzo sits up. 'Sap. Bet she's terrified I'm going to report her to Mr Regan.'

'Why is she even in our house?' Orla asks.

'I guess she's friends with Joy and the others,' Chloe says.

Izzo scoffs. 'Doubt it. Who'd want to be friends with her? She's easily the weirdest person in our year.'

'She's the weirdest person in the whole school,' Orla adds.

I'm surprised she has so many opinions on the matter.

'I don't know,' Izzo says. 'Leslie Park is full of weirdos. Like those creepy twins in Fourth Year who wear their hair in matching plaits and sing at the school masses.'

'Or that First Year who wears earmuffs indoors,' Orla says.

Izzo laughs. 'OK, she's definitely the weirdest person in our school. I saw her shouting at a Fifth Year for knocking into her in the stairs once. A *Fifth* Year.'

'I feel like that girl's actually different though,' Chloe says. 'Like, I think she might have autism.'

I start at the mention of the word and sit on my hands to steady myself.

'See,' Izzo says. 'Weirdo.'

'Hey!' Chloe snaps. 'You know my cousin has autism.'

'Yeah, but he's adorable. This girl is, like, possessed or something.'

'And she smells so badly of B.O.' Orla adds.

I get up quickly and go to the bathroom before my body starts reacting involuntarily to this conversation.

Oh, God, I think as I sit on the edge of the bath and press my palms onto my face. *Is this what people think about me?* Memories of the many times teachers have singled me out in class litter my head; the times Orla looked mortified to even know me at lunch time, let alone be my friend. Was I as weird to everyone as that First Year? Snow swirls around and around in my belly. I have to contain it. I wipe my eyes coarsely with my sleeve and try to shake the fuzzy feeling off my skin.

Back in the room, I am relieved to hear that the conversation has moved on. I pay close attention to how everyone is sitting and try my best to blend in. I tuck one leg behind the other, like Chloe, and bunch my hands in the pouch of my hoodie like Izzo. *Be normal*, I scold myself.

'So, what's everyone wearing tonight?' Izzo asks.

'Ugh, I'm so not bothered getting dressed up for a *céilí*,' Chloe says.

'It's not like there's anything else to do,' Izzo replies. She glances around the room. 'Freya, let me do your make-up.'

My eyes round in alarm. Was this some sort of trick? I'm glad she can't see me clasping my hands together in my pocket.

'Freya?' Izzo says.

Be fun and easy-going.

'Sure,' I squeak.

Izzo grins. 'Amazing. We can use my stuff.'

She slides down from her bunk and takes a large, pastel-coloured pouch from her suitcase.

'Here, put this on,' she instructs, passing me a headband and plonking the pouch on my bed. She rummages through its contents, pulls out a tube of foundation and pumps a small amount onto her fingertips. She spreads it across my forehead and cheekbones with an egg-shaped sponge, which I recognise from the Zoe Turner tutorials. I seize the opportunity to impress her straight away.

'I think Zoe Turner has a sponge like this,' I say as casually as I can.

Izzo flips her hair over her shoulder. 'Oh my God, I'm obsessed with Zoe Turner.'

She continues to sweep and dot various powders and liquids across my face, expertly alternating between make-up brushes and her fingertips. At first I flinch at her touch, but the pads of her fingers are soft and pleasantly cool, and she is less terrifying when concentrating.

'Whoa, Freya,' Chloe says, looking up from her phone after Izzo declares my make-over complete. 'You're *hot*. You should wear make-up more often.'

Izzo flips open a small mirror for me to look at myself.

Even I'm surprised by the results. I still look like me, but a more grown up, Instagram me. I'm tempted to touch my face, but don't want to mess up Izzo's work. 'Thanks, Izzo,' I say.

'No prob,' she replies, packing up her things. 'You honestly look so pretty. Here, you can keep this.' She tosses a small, half-empty tub of highlighter at me. 'It's perfect on you and I hardly use it anyway.'

'You really do look so pretty, Freya,' Chloe says, smiling. I feel myself blushing and instinctively look over at Orla. She glances at me for a second, before burying her face in her phone again.

Izzo pats the seat next to her on the bus. 'Freya, sit beside me.'
She and Chloe are on the three-seater at the back, and when I
take my seat, Orla is forced to sit on her own. I hadn't planned
on sitting here, but I feel indebted to Izzo now that she's done
my make-up and given me a gift.

It's dusk by the time we reach the community centre, and a
gang of local teenage boys have congregated outside to watch
us descend from the bus. One of them wolf whistles as we
walk by. The sound cuts through my ear canal, and I try not to
flinch. Izzo links arms with me, a gesture that makes me tense
and jittery at once.

'Creeps,' she scoffs as we pass the boys, while waving
flirtatiously in their direction. 'Bet they're all inbred.'

We take our seats along the benches in the hall, and Izzo
turns towards me so that our knees are touching. She picks
bits of lint from my hoodie and plays with the ends of my hair.
I don't know what's changed, but it's like I'm her doll all of a
sudden, or maybe her pet. Chloe sits down beside us, clearly
unfazed by the shift in dynamic in the group. Orla, meanwhile,
watches Izzo and me intently from the corner of her eye.

Nóirín and the other teachers stand in the middle of the hall
and get our attention.

'We're going to learn a few dances tonight, *a chailíní*,' Nóirín announces, rubbing her hands together like she's lathering them with soap. 'We'll start with a dance called *Ballaí Luimnigh*. I want everyone to find a partner and organise yourselves into groups of four.'

'Freya,' Izzo says, reaching for my hand. 'Partners?'

I can hardly refuse her.

We watch the teachers as they demonstrate the steps (Mr Regan is a concerning shade of crimson by the end), then organise ourselves into rows of two. Chloe and Orla stand in front of Izzo and me, their hands clasped in preparation for the music. I pretend not to notice the scowl on Orla's face.

We perform the dance a few times until most of us are out of breath. I'm relieved when Nóirín finally turns the music off and instructs us to take our seats again.

'The next dance we're going to learn is *Cur Crúb ar an Asal*,' she announces. She and Michelle demonstrate the steps for us, pacing back and forth across the floor and changing direction in time with the music. When they call us back to the floor and tell us to arrange ourselves in a big circle, I notice that my partner is missing and scan the hall for her. Did Izzo go to the bathroom? She was taking a long time, if she did. I linger at the sidelines while the other girls organise themselves, and when the music starts and Izzo still hasn't returned, I take a seat on one of the benches.

'Oh, no you don't,' Nóirín says, spotting me and pulling me to my feet. 'I've a partner over here for you.'

She takes me by the arm and leads me to Shannon, who is also partnerless, and has been dancing with Michelle until now.

'I should warn you,' Shannon says, taking my hand. 'I'm not particularly co-ordinated.'

The steps of the dance are neat and quick and before we know it, our cheeks are flushed, our hands slipping with sweat as we turn repeatedly on our heels in time with the music.

'They've tricked us into exercising,' Shannon says, doubled over and panting when Nóirín finally hits stop. 'If I wanted to exercise, I wouldn't have quit hockey after First Year. Hey, you look really nice by the way.'

I touch my face self-consciously. 'Izzo's idea.'

Shannon grimaces at the mention of her name. 'Is she still mad at me? She didn't seem to take my apology very well. I feel bad. I should've just ignored her. I mean, I actually did have my period, but I didn't want to give her the satisfaction of being right. Ugh, I'm an idiot.'

I don't tell Shannon that I think a slice of ham to the face was the least Izzo deserved last night and that I admire her for actually having the courage to be angry, instead of squashing all her feelings inside herself.

'So, tomorrow we're going on that fairy walk. Think we'll accidentally stumble across any orgies?' Shannon says.

'I hope not,' I say, shuddering, and we both laugh.

When Izzo finally returns to the hall, she has a huge grin on her face and searches frantically for Chloe and Orla. She whispers something to them and the three of them begin squealing excitedly.

'Did she learn to go to the toilet by herself or something?' Shannon says.

I laugh weakly as I watch them, tired already for the night ahead.

Chapter 16

'He's not even that hot,' Izzo says, engrossed by her phone. 'But he asked for my number, so whatever.'

The three of them are sitting on Izzo's top bunk, their faces pressed together to see her screen more closely. I pretend to organise my suitcase on the far side of the room.

'He's not bad,' Chloe says, tilting her head.

'He's definitely the best looking one,' Orla says.

They're discussing the group of boys outside the community centre this evening. One of them called Izzo over as she was making her way to the bathroom, and she hung out with them in the carpark while the rest of us sweated it out in the dance hall. She exchanged phone numbers and Instagram handles with a guy called Jack, and now grids are being scrutinised.

'Oh crap, he's messaging me!' Izzo squeals, sitting back and pulling her phone from view of the others.

'What's he saying?' Orla asks excitedly.

'Nothing,' Izzo says, suddenly secretive. 'Oh God. He wants a selfie. I already took my make-up off.'

'Just send an old one,' Chloe suggests.

Izzo says nothing as she types quickly, a giddy glint in her eye.

'He wants to see you guys!' she says. 'Quick, let me take a picture.' She holds her phone in front of Orla and Chloe.

'No way, I took my make-up off too,' Orla says.

'You look fine,' Izzo replies.

'No, I'm serious. Don't take a photo, Izzo.'

'Oh, relax. He just wants to see what we're up to. Ready? One, two, three, *smile*!'

'Izzo!' Orla shrieks, lunging for Izzo's phone. 'Don't send that!'

'Oops, too late.'

'Izzo, what the ...'

Orla's fuming. I can hear it in her voice. But her words trail off, her better judgement swooping in before she makes the mistake of challenging Izzo. I watch as she decides to drop the argument.

'You looked gorgeous, honestly,' Izzo says sweetly. 'I wouldn't have sent it otherwise.'

'What's he saying?' Chloe says impatiently. 'Has he seen it?'

'He... he wants to know who's in the background. Freya, he means you! Here, let me get a better shot.' Izzo leans over the side of the bunk. 'Smile!'

I stare ahead like a startled animal, a pair of socks hanging limply in my hand.

'Well?' Chloe says. 'What's he saying now?'

'He says…' Izzo waits for the message to come in. 'He says that he thinks Freya's cute! He's going to show his friends our photos.'

Orla scrambles down from the bed, grabs her wash bag and leaves the room. I notice that her cheeks are wet as she passes by.

'What's her problem?' Izzo says, briefly looking up from her phone before getting distracted by it again.

I take my wash bag and follow her out.

A strip of light frames the bathroom door at the end of the dark corridor. I walk towards it and knock gently.

'Just a sec.' Orla's voice is thick with emotion. She blows her nose loudly.

'It's me,' I say.

'Who?'

'Freya.'

Silence.

The door opens and Orla brushes past me, her cheeks red and irritated. 'All yours,' she says, without looking at me.

'Are you OK?' I ask.

'Fine.' Her voice is tight.

'Really? You don't seem…'

'Why can't you just leave me alone? It's like you're always following me.'

She storms back to the room, her bare feet making a sticky sound against the tiles.

Chapter 17

'They say the mere sight of a *púca* is enough to prevent a hen from laying eggs or a cow from giving milk ever again,' P.J., the local historian tells us, raising a cautioning finger. We're standing in a circle in the middle of a field, listening to him as he tells us about different kinds of fairies in Ireland.

'It takes many forms to disguise itself, and around these parts, you know you've found one when you encounter a black goat with curling horns. In this form, the *púca* roams the countryside, tearing down fences and gates at night, scattering livestock and trampling crops. It's a vindictive fairy, as they go, and if you ignore it when it summons you, it'll vandalise your property!'

'So cool,' Shannon whispers beside me. 'Irish fairies are *way* more badass than Disney ones.'

I ignore this comment. I'm only trailing behind Shannon because the tension between my roommates is too crackly to bear. I also don't want to risk annoying Orla more than I already have, so am trying to give her space.

We start walking across the field, and it's clear that Shannon and I are the only ones paying any real attention to P.J. as he continues to tell us about fairies. The other girls link arms in twos and threes around us and talk among themselves, lowering their English-speaking voices whenever Mr Regan or one of the other teachers passes by. Orla, Izzo, and Chloe are somewhere near the back and I glance back on occasion to see what they're doing. Izzo's hands are firmly bunched in the pockets of her puffer, while Chloe and Orla link arms together. Orla's been peddling the lie that she has a headache today, rather than admitting that she's upset with Izzo. Izzo isn't paying her much attention either way.

'And over here,' P.J. says, pointing to the ruin of a farmhouse, 'the cruellest act a fairy can commit was carried out long ago. A little baby was snatched from her cradle one night and replaced with a changeling. Now, changelings may look human on the outside, but they're really fairies in disguise, and they wreak havoc wherever they go.'

'Come on,' Shannon says, grabbing my arm. 'I want to find out more.'

She drags me towards P.J. and we step in line with him as he walks.

'What happened to the little girl?' Shannon asks. 'Did the fairies ever give her back?'

'It wouldn't have been in their interest,' P.J. says. 'They'd have taken the child in the first place to strengthen their own stock, or maybe out of revenge or spite. You never know with fairies.'

'How did the parents know that their baby had been replaced in the first place? What did the changeling do?'

'Changelings were said to have cried a lot and were often sickly and irritable old things. They couldn't be taught to do much and were always causing their poor parents' grief. Of course, they do say nowadays that changelings were probably just people with disabilities and the like. The poor lass in the house over probably just had a touch of the… what do they call it… the autism.'

I force a neutral expression and hope the panic clattering around inside me doesn't register on my face. That word. It's like it's haunting me. I don't speak for the rest of the walk, and focus instead on squashing down whatever emotions P.J.'s story has stirred in me.

That evening, Orla lies curled on her bed while Izzo messages Jack on the bunk above. I search for a playlist to help me feel as far away from this psychedelic fish tank as possible.

'What're you listening to, Freya?' Chloe asks. I'd forgotten she was even here.

'Disney playlist,' I say, to my immediate regret. I had created a fake playlist with normal music on it to mention if ever the topic came up.

But Chloe doesn't laugh or smirk. She looks genuinely interested. 'Which film?'

'Just different Pixar ones,' I say.

'Can I listen?'

She takes a seat at the edge of my bed. I tentatively give her my headphones.

'This song is so cute. What is it?'

'*Lava*. It's from one of the short films.'

'I'm definitely learning this on the ukulele.'

Thinking about conversation tennis, I'm about to ask Chloe about the ukulele when Izzo interrupts.

'Oh my *God*,' she squeals, scrambling upright on her bunk. 'Jack and his friends want to meet us outside the community centre tonight!'

'Are you serious?' Chloe says, dropping my headphones and clambering onto Izzo's bunk. 'What did you say?' I can't tell from her tone whether she's excited or concerned about this development. I hope it's the latter.

'*Yes*, obviously!' Izzo says. 'We can sneak out during the table quiz.'

'Won't it be obvious if we're all on the same team and our table is empty?' Orla says, her headache miraculously disappeared.

'True,' Izzo says, thinking. 'We can split up and go on different teams so nobody notices. It'll be easy. Oh, and *Freya*,' she adds in a singsong voice. 'Jack says his friend Burns really liked that photo of you. He can't wait to meet you later. Here, I'll do your make-up again.'

The room quickly fills with clashing smells of hairspray and deodorant, powders and lotions, and I stifle multiple sneezes as Izzo fusses over my eyebrows.

'How many of them are there?' Orla wants to know.

'I don't know, five maybe? One for each of us anyway.'

I want to ask what we'll do outside the community centre, and what exactly *one for each of us* means, but it's all I can do to keep my breathing steady as Izzo's face hovers mere inches from my own. Tonight we were meeting *boys*.

Chapter 18

Splitting up for the evening proves a great idea, and I'm grateful for the break from my roommates ahead of Izzo's plans for later. We're all in the hall for the table quiz, and I'm sitting with Shannon, Joy, Fatimah and Eva.

'Team name ideas?' Joy says, tapping her pencil against a blank sheet of paper.

'Something clever,' Eva says.

'Is that a suggestion?' Shannon asks.

'What? No, I mean pick something clever! Something with a pun in it or something.'

'I don't know, I kind of like Something Clever as a name,' Fatimah says.

'Works for me,' Joy says. 'But I'm going to translate it into Irish. There might be bonus points.'

'Got to love her competitive streak,' Fatimah says teasingly.

Around the hall, Izzo, Chloe and Orla sit at different tables and glance at each other every other minute.

'I thought they were inseparable,' Shannon remarks.

I don't respond.

The quiz begins and the first round is all about fairies.

'Let's see who was paying attention on our walk today,' Nóirín says, grinning.

'So they're tricking us into an exam,' Eva says, unimpressed.

'Tricking us into exams, into exercise. I'm telling you, there's a hidden agenda at this so-called Irish College,' Shannon says.

From the corner of my eye, I see Izzo slink out of the hall and into the corridor. Chloe follows a few minutes later, then Orla. Nobody seems to notice them except me. I start to feel distracted then, wondering if they're expecting me outside, or if I've missed my cue to join them. A prickling sensation begins to creep over my skin.

Chloe reappears at the door and takes the long route back to her table so that she can pass by ours.

'Freya, Izzo wants you for a second,' she whispers.

'Well, that was weird,' Shannon says after Chloe takes her seat again. 'Why does Izzo want you?'

I shrug and rise unsteadily to my feet.

Outside, I hear them before I see them, and follow the sound of laughter and chatter around the side of the building. It takes my eyes a moment to adjust to the darkness, but then I see that they are huddled together by a low wall, their outlines blurred into one dark blob.

'Finally!' Izzo says. She's sitting on Jack's lap; he's sitting on the wall, his arms loosely wrapped around her waist. Next to them, Orla appears to be in a play fight with another guy, who has taken the plastic claw from her hair and is pretending to attack her with it. She is all shrieks and giggles, sounds I've never heard her make before. Two other guys lean against the wall opposite them.

'You've kept poor Burns waiting,' Izzo says, her voice syrupy and adult-like. She gestures towards one of the leaning guys, who stands with his hands bunched in the pouch of his hoodie and his head down.

'All right?' he says, glancing up briefly before returning his gaze to the gravel under our feet.

I don't respond, just stand there with my arms crossed and try to keep my body still. This is already too much.

'Does she talk, or what?' Jack says, watching me.

'She's just shy,' Izzo responds, playfully slapping his arm. 'Isn't that right, Freya?'

I don't say anything.

'Shy or slow?' the guy next to Burns says, and they all laugh. Even Orla.

Izzo pretends to be offended on my behalf, and extends a leg to kick him.

'What?' he says. 'She's the one standing there like a space cadet.'

Orla's guy steps in front of me then and waves her hair claw in my face. 'Yoohoo,' he says in a stupid puppet voice.

'Anyone in there?'

The suggestion that I'm somehow not here makes me bristle. People had a tendency to talk about me this way. *In a world of her own. Away with the fairies. Head in the clouds.* Roundabout ways of saying that I'm disconnected from the world, even though I'm here, I'm more here than most people seem to be. Why else did I find noise so loud, light so bright, smell so strong, touch so intense? Other people could tune these things out, but I… I shake the thoughts from my head. Now is not the time for getting distracted, not when these guys have already clocked my oddness.

'Is she deaf or something?' one of them says.

Orla's guy inches closer to me, still using the claw as a puppet, and I feel my chest closing in on itself.

My whole body feels fuzzy now, behind my ears and my fingertips tingling. *I'm not safe, I'm not safe.* He leans in and grabs my nose with it, the plastic teeth scraping painfully across my skin. I smack his arm away forcefully and it hits the wall. The hair claw breaks in two. My reaction surprises me and my hands are really trembling now.

'Fuckin' hell,' the guy says, apparently … impressed? 'No messin' with you, like!'

'Go, Freya!' Izzo says. 'Show that prick who's boss.'

'That'll teach ya, Darren,' Jack says.

'Sorry about your hair yoke,' Darren says to Orla, throwing

the pieces in her direction.

'Whatever,' she says, kicking them away from her. 'Was just cheap crap anyway.'

She doesn't mean that. I can hear it in her voice that she's annoyed.

Around the corner, I hear footsteps on the gravel. The others don't seem to notice. 'Someone's coming,' I say urgently.

'*Fuuuuuck*,' Izzo mouths, although she appears excited by the prospect.

'Ye go around the building the back way,' Jack says. 'We'll distract.'

Izzo, Orla and I run. We are halfway around the back of the building when I hear Nóirín interrogate the boys and threaten to call their parents if they don't clear off the grounds immediately.

We make it around to the other side unnoticed and quickly bundle inside the main door. Izzo and Orla compose themselves before returning to the hall, but I make a turn for the bathroom.

I slide the latch across a cubicle door and lower myself to my hunkers. My heart is rattling like a cartoon alarm clock in my chest, my hands and hairline damp with sweat. I try to breathe deeply, but every breath feels like it's caught on barbed wire. *Not now*, I beg my body as I feel myself lose control. *Please not now.* But the tears fall anyway, and my arms and legs start to shake. I clumsily pull streams of toilet paper from the dispenser on the wall, gather it like a paper cloud and press my face into it. I give into my jagged breathing then, let myself cry.

It's too much to follow my plan to get Orla and the others to like me when my head is stuffed up with so many other things. My too-hard pillow and scratchy bed sheets. The bubble wallpaper that makes me feel trapped underwater. The bright, echoey classroom that hurts my eyes and ears. Jackie's watchful eye at mealtimes. Changelings. Izzo and these guys. It's impossible to ignore them because they're all happening at once.

I dry my face and shake out my hands and legs to speed up the process of feeling somewhat normal again. Thank God for bathroom cubicles.

A knock sounds on the door and I start. I look down and recognise the flowery boots on the other side.

'Freya? Is that you? Are you OK?' Shannon says.

Why does Shannon have to be here right now? I stand up and pull back the latch, march past her to the sink.

'Oh my God, Freya. What happened?' she says, looking over my shoulder in the mirror. 'Did you have a panic attack? Can I help?'

I don't care that she can see my red-rimmed eyes and blotchy cheeks. She's the one who barged in on me when I was trying to calm down. 'Why can't you just leave me alone?' I say, and push my way past her. 'It's like you're always following me.' I say it coldly, just like Orla did to me.

Back in the hall, Shannon quietly takes her seat at our table and doesn't look at me.

'We came in joint third,' Joy tells her, disappointed. 'If we had just known the name of that stupid reindeer from *Frozen*...'

They didn't know Sven?! I don't say anything, just look down at my lap and hope my hair hides the state of my face right now.

Chapter 19

'Y ou should have seen Freya,' Izzo tells Chloe in our room. 'Darren was being a total dick to her and she just annihilated him. It was so funny.'

I'm stunned that *this* is how the story is being told, that I've not only gotten away with what I did, but even earned kudos from Izzo in the process.

'I can't believe you guys almost got caught,' Chloe says. 'I was going to go back outside, but then I saw Nóirín heading out and got too freaked out.'

'Thank God Freya heard her coming,' Izzo says. 'We were *this* close to getting caught.'

'I was so afraid Nóirín was going to find my hair claw,' Orla says. 'It was still on the ground from after Freya smacked it out of Darren's hand.'

'Still can't believe you did that, Freya,' Chloe says. 'So funny.'

I still can't believe that they think me losing control was me taking control. They don't know what happened in the bathroom cubicle afterwards. Only Shannon saw that part.

The next day, the teachers cut our final afternoon class short to bring us to the beach. I'm glad to be out of our classroom, but I wish I had my earmuffs to stop the wind from whistling through my ear canals.

'I can't believe they thought this was a good idea,' Izzo says, shivering next to me on the sand dunes. 'It's actually unreasonable how windy it is today.'

'Great drying weather,' I say absently, staring out at the sea.

Izzo snorts. 'Oh my God, Freya, you sound like my nana.'

I wince. I should know better than to use small talk I've learned from Mum in conversation with people my own age. 'I was obviously joking,' I say in my best Izzo voice.

Further ahead, Shannon and her roommates are having a competition to see who can moonwalk the fastest to the water. At one point, Joy is winning and Shannon and Fatimah team up to hold her back so that Eva gets to the finish line first. Eva lifts her arms up and runs up and down the shore in victory as the others laugh. I feel a slight pull towards them. They had saved a seat for me on the bus this morning, but I'd sat with Izzo instead. I still haven't spoken to Shannon since last night.

After dinner, we lie on our beds and scroll through our phones.

'Oh my God! Oh my *God*,' Izzo squeals suddenly, swinging her legs over the edge of her bunk. 'Jack wants us to sneak out tonight. He says they can collect us after we get back from the *céilí* and drive us to some place called The Castle. He says he and the guys bought fireworks for Halloween and we can set them off!'

'Ugh, I don't know,' Chloe says. 'It'll be freezing and we'll get in so much trouble if we get caught.'

'Oh, come on, Clo. Cauley will be there. You know he likes you, and he hardly got to see you last night.'

Chloe shoves a handful of vegan Percy Pigs in her mouth, her chewing not quite masking her smiling.

'And Darren *officially* likes Orla,' Izzo continues. 'Jack told me.'

'Really?' Orla says, emerging from her bottom bunk like a little animal.

Izzo shrugs teasingly. 'See, we *have* to go. It'll be fun.'

'Who's going to drive?' Chloe asks. 'Aren't they all our age?'

'Burns has his licence. He'll drive, but only if Freya comes too.' She says it as if I'm not in the room.

'Do you want to come, Freya?' Chloe asks.

Izzo looks at me. 'You're definitely coming, aren't you, Freya?'

'Yeah, please, Freya,' Orla says. It's hard to believe the imploring look in her eyes.

'Yeah,' I say limply, my lips not even moving. *Be fun. Be normal.*

'Amazing! Freya, you're the best. Orla, can I borrow your

black Hollister hoodie?' Izzo asks, swiftly moving on with her plans.

Orla looks panicked. 'I was going to wear it.'

'Really? But you said I could wear it one of the nights.'

'I know, but then you never asked for it.'

'But I'm asking now. Please? Tonight's *so* important. I think Jack's going to shift me.'

'Oh,' Orla says weakly. 'OK.'

'Thanks *so* much, Orla. You can borrow any of my clothes.'

I pretend to scroll through my phone as the others apply make-up, straighten their hair and change from one set of high-waisted leggings and hoodies into another.

'I love that scent,' Chloe says, sniffing the air.

'Zoe Turner. So nice, isn't it?' Izzo replies.

The sickly-sweet smell catches in the back of my throat and I cough.

'Freya, you should wear some of the highlighter I gave you,' Izzo suggests, looking at me through the mirror on the wall as she brushes her hair. 'It's so pretty on you.'

I obediently retrieve the metallic tub from my wash bag and begin to apply it in the small mirror in the lid.

'Do you really want to come, Freya?' Chloe asks again.

'Yeah,' I squeak, and look over at Orla, who is wearing Izzo's dinner-stained hoodie and busy applying lashings of mascara to her eyelashes, her tongue poking out of the side of her mouth as she concentrates. 'It'll be fun!' I add in Izzo's voice. I return my focus to applying highlighter and try to ignore the rumbling snowglobe in my stomach.

Chapter 20

Izzo paces impatiently as the other girls continue their supper. 'Are they being this slow on purpose? Seriously.'

We arrived home tonight to a spread of biscuits, mini muffins and hot chocolate in the dining room. Jackie told us we'd been great guests and to enjoy our last night in the house. While the other girls were doing exactly that, Izzo, Chloe, Orla and I slipped back to our room on Izzo's cue.

Eventually we hear the scrape of chairs against tiles and the girls heading back to their rooms. There are further delays in the corridor as they take turns in the bathroom, but soon the house is quiet. Jackie peeps into every room to say *oíche mhaith* for the last time and make sure we're all in bed. When she switches off the light in the corridor, I know that it's time for the next phase of the night. I scrunch my toes and squeeze them hard underneath the duvet.

'Finally,' Izzo says, stripping back her duvet. She is, as we all are, dressed and ready to go. 'Come on. They'll be here soon.'

We organise ourselves in a single file, our shoes in our hands so that we don't make noise tiptoeing along the corridor. Izzo leads the way to the front door, which she inspected earlier and discovered could be unlocked without a key from the inside.

The night is cool and clear, with white stars studding the sky overhead. The lack of street lights in the area means there are more stars than I am used to seeing, and I can't help craning my neck back and gazing up at them, mesmerised by their clarity and abundance.

'Hurry up,' Izzo hisses, prompting me to catch up with the others. I stuff my feet into my runners and go.

I'm squinting to see them in the inky darkness, when suddenly a glaringly bright sensor light illuminates the entire garden, exposing us completely.

'Quick!' Izzo whispers, racing to the top of the drive. She ducks behind the wall beside the gate and we bundle in beside her, breathless, like stowaways.

'That was close,' Chloe says, clapping a hand over her mouth to stop herself from laughing.

'Do you think anyone noticed?' Orla says.

'Nah. They'll think it was a cow or something,' Izzo assures her, even though we haven't seen any cows in Slievanure so far. She takes out her phone and starts messaging Jack.

'Are they close, or what?' Chloe asks. 'I'm already freezing.'

'Almost here. Burns was late collecting them.'

I wince at the mention of his name, scrunch my toes inside my runners and squeeze my fists into balls inside my pockets.

Over the hill, a stream of light spills onto the road and a car winds its way towards us. It pulls up just a few feet from the drive and we follow Izzo as she crouches down and scurries towards it.

Jack winds down his window in the front passenger seat. 'Well, how are ye doing?' he says, grinning as we hug ourselves in the cold.

'Can you just let us in? It's freezing out here,' Izzo says impatiently.

Jack steps out and opens the back door of the car, where Cauley and Darren are seated. 'Come on,' he says, squeezing in beside them. 'You'll have to sit on our laps, but Ariel can sit up front.' He points to me and winks.

'What? Who's Ariel?' Izzo says.

'Like the Little Mermaid.'

Izzo snorts. 'You're such a weirdo.'

'What? I just seen Kylie Jenner dressed up as that for Halloween. Better than the Little Mute, ha?' He winks at me again.

The backseat passengers quickly arrange themselves, and I reluctantly sit in the front seat. At least I'm not on anyone's lap.

'Well,' Burns grunts, quickly glancing at me as he starts the car.

I turn my whole body away from him.

'That was close!' Izzo says as we take off. 'Can you imagine if we got caught just now? We'd be so screwed! So, where are we going? It better not be some stupid bog.'

'Very rude,' Jack says, feigning offence. 'Slievanure's our home.'

'Yeah,' Cauley adds. 'Beautiful part of the world. Ye Dublin girls don't appreciate it.'

'Oh, please,' Izzo scoffs. 'We're the most exciting thing that's happened to this dump in years.'

Burns stops the car at the foot of a hill and we all step out. There's a ruin at the top, shadowy and ominous under the moonlight. Perfect for Halloween, except everything about tonight is unsettling enough without added effects. We all stand around, our arms wrapped tightly around ourselves for warmth.

Jack pulls a glass bottle from the pouch of his hoodie. 'Tipple, anyone?'

'Good man, Jack,' Darren says, clapping him on the back.

'Give it here,' Izzo demands, twisting the red cap off and taking a swig of the clear liquid. Her face contorts as she swallows, and she passes the bottle to Chloe. Chloe takes a mouthful and gulps loudly before passing the bottle to Orla. The bottle eventually makes its way back to Jack, who passes it to me.

'Your turn,' he says, thrusting the almost empty bottle in front of me.

My arms remain tightly crossed. I shake my head.

'Ah, come on. Would you just take a sip, would you?'

I don't respond.

'It's not that bad,' Orla says. 'Honestly.'

I catch her eye and she actually smiles at me.

I take the bottle from Jack. The stench of its contents catches in my nostrils before I even lift it to my mouth. I tilt my head back and bring the bottle to my lips gingerly. A small stream of liquid snakes down my tongue, burning off a layer of it as it goes. By the time it reaches my throat, I'm certain my whole head is going to catch fire. I shudder audibly after swallowing, causing the others to laugh.

'Nice one,' Cauley says, nudging me in the arm.

'So, what exactly are we doing here?' Chloe asks, looking around.

'We're going to climb to the top of the hill,' Jack says. 'It's pretty nice up there. You can see the sea under the moonlight.'

'How romantic,' Izzo says dryly.

'Will be when we get the fireworks going.'

Izzo rolls her eyes. 'Yeah, because Halloween is famously the most romantic night of the year.'

'What's the story anyway? Did ye not think to bring Halloween costumes on your little trip?'

'Yeah,' Cauley says. 'No little bunny ears or anything?'

'If we were at home we'd have dressed up,' Chloe says, 'but we didn't think we'd be doing anything here.'

'Oh yeah, and what would you have gone as at home then?'

'Definitely not bunnies,' Izzo says.

'What about you, Ariel?' He turns and looks at me.

'Hei Hei,' I say quietly.

'What?'

'The rooster from *Moana*?' Orla says.

They all burst out laughing and I realise I shouldn't have said anything.

'A fuckin' rooster!' Jack says. 'That's bloody brilliant. You're a gas one, Ariel.'

'Can we start the fireworks now?' Izzo says.

'Race you up the hill,' Jack says.

Izzo runs ahead and Jack chases after her. The others follow suit and I notice Darren draping his arm over Orla as they climb.

'Come on,' Burns says to me, extending his hand.

I ignore him and start walking towards the others.

He catches up and walks beside me. I feel his arm wander across my back. I try to shrug him away, walk faster up the hill, but he hooks his arm around my waist and pulls me back in.

'What's up with you anyway?' he says, stopping me in my tracks, both hands firmly clamped on my hips so that I can't get away. 'Always playing hard to get.'

His hands inch around to the small of my back. 'You're so pretty, like,' he tells me, leaning in towards my face with horrible hot breath. His hands have now crept under the back of my hoodie and I flinch as his icy fingers stroke my bare skin. 'Come on,' he says, cocking his head to the side and leaning in closer. 'Just a little kiss.'

I want to say no. I want to scream the word in his face. But it won't come, and all I can do is shake my head repeatedly. I turn my face away from him, but he steers it back with his hand and holds my jaw in place. He leans in to kiss me again and this time plants his mouth on mine. I breathe through my nose, quick, shallow breaths as his horrible tongue attacks me and his stubbly chin rubs against my skin like sandpaper. I look at the stars over his shoulder. They blur into a milky mass as my eyes fill with tears.

'Woooo!' Izzo calls from the top of the hill, 'Get it, Freya!'

'Go on, Burns, you beast!' Jack shouts.

We both look up at the cluster of figures at the top of the hill, and with Burns' hands momentarily lifted in distraction, I run. I do it without thinking, without looking back. I run down the hill, past the car, down the road, past the fields. I run until my chest is burning, my temples are throbbing and my legs are trembling. My breath is ragged and desperate, my throat shredded by the cold, but I keep running until I am back inside the house.

Chapter 21

I am clumsy with the handle of our bedroom door, louder than I mean to be opening it, but unable to steady my shaking hands enough to be quiet.

'Freya? What are you doing?' Shannon stands behind me, her wash bag in hand, a pillowy packet of sanitary pads sticking out of it. I'm not mad at her for finding me this time. I'm relieved that she's here.

She follows me into the room. 'What's going on? Where is everyone?' she asks, taking in the empty beds. I don't respond, just sit on the edge of my bed trembling and trying to catch my breath.

'Oh my God, you're freezing,' Shannon says, touching my hand with the back of hers. 'What... what happened?'

I screw my eyes shut and try to organise my thoughts. 'The hill,' I say, spitting out the words as quickly as I can before they dissolve on my tongue. 'Boys drove.'

Shannon tries to piece together this information. 'Boys drove you... to a hill?'

I nod urgently.

'What? Why?'

My tongue feels heavy in my mouth, but I force the words out. 'Izzo. Jack. Fireworks.'

Shannon shakes her head in confusion. 'Freya, I have no idea what you're talking about. Can you give me a little more information?'

I feel myself begin to cry again and press my palms over my eyes to stop the tears.

'Are you having another panic attack?' Shannon asks. 'That's what it looked like yesterday, but I wasn't—'

I shake my head.

'OK, well maybe your body is having some kind of reaction to something. My brother's diabetic and when his blood sugar's low he gets—'

'I'm autistic,' I blurt.

Shannon's eyebrows lift in surprise, but she doesn't say anything.

I wipe my nose with my hand. 'I'm not having a panic attack,' I say with a croaky voice. 'I just… I get overwhelmed sometimes and I can't cope and then I lose control for a bit.'

My voice catches as I speak, but I'm amazed at my ability to put words to my experience, to coherently explain what is happening. I've never done that before.

'Oh, Freya,' Shannon says. 'I'm sorry. That sounds so scary.'

I feel myself recoil a bit then, like the moment is somehow

too real. 'Nobody else knows,' I say. 'It's not something–'

Before I can finish my sentence, the bedroom door swings open and a stream of light spills in from the corridor.

'What in the name of God is going on here?' Jackie demands, frantically tying a lipstick-patterned dressing gown around her waist. Shannon and I look at each other.

'Where are the rest of them?' she says, registering the three empty beds. 'And don't even think about lying to me. I've already checked, and I know the front door's unlocked. They've gone out, haven't they?' She huffs loudly. 'Every bloody year, I swear to God.'

Shannon stands up. 'They went out with… local guys. I think they… collected them in a car and drove to a hill.' She looks at me for confirmation and I nod. Her voice is remarkably calm as she speaks, and I'm grateful that she's here.

Jackie is seething. 'I'm calling that teacher of yours,' she says, pulling her phone from her pocket. 'He can deal with this. Where did they go?'

Shannon and Jackie both look at me. If I could unscrew the top of my head and show them what I know it would be easier. Far easier than trying to shape thoughts into words, which requires far more skill than I'm capable of right now. 'The Castle,' I manage weakly.

Jackie's phone is pressed to her ear as she shakes her head in disgust. 'Brendan, hi. It's Jackie Walsh here. Look, I'm after waking to find a group of them – how many?' Shannon holds up three fingers. 'Three of them have gone out with a group of young fellas from the village. They've gone up to the old castle. Yeah, yeah. I know. Right. I'll see you then.'

Jackie huffs loudly. 'The little wagons. I swear to God if they cost me my job…' Her eyes narrow suddenly as she registers what I'm wearing. 'Were you out with them?'

I nod. She is so terrifying right now that it doesn't even occur to me to lie.

'Don't you nod your head like that at me. Tell me, were you with them?'

I look at Shannon, who gives a small, helpless smile. 'Yes,' I say.

'Look at me, for God's sake, would you?'

I force myself to lock eyes with her. It makes my whole body tense. Eye contact was difficult enough without a fuming Jackie on the other end of it.

The sensor lights come on outside and a car pulls into the drive. We follow Jackie to the hall and stand back as she opens the front door to Mr Regan. His hair is unkempt, and he's wearing a tracksuit. It is surreal seeing a teacher at this hour of the night.

'Tell me this second what's gone on here tonight,' Mr Regan says, holding up an accusatory finger at Shannon and me.

'Izzo, Chloe and Orla went out with a group of guys and

drove to a castle, I think,' Shannon says.

'It's a bit of a hot spot for the young ones,' Jackie explains.

'Which boys? Where did they meet boys?'

Shannon looks at me. If she could answer for me, I know she would.

'The community centre,' I manage, consciously trying to project my voice so that I won't be asked to repeat myself. 'Izzo was talking to one of them.'

Mr Regan huffs at the mention of Izzo's name. 'I should've known. Right, I'm going out looking for them. Jackie, can you tell me which direction to go?'

'This one can tell you,' she says, pointing to me. 'She was with them.'

Mr Regan's mouth opens slightly. 'Freya?' he says. 'Right. You're going to have to come and direct me. Shannon, you'd better come, too. Jackie, I am so sorry about all of this. We'll be back shortly.'

'Oh, I'll be waiting,' Jackie says. 'They won't be going to bed without getting past me first.'

Mr Regan's car is cold and smells of mucky football boots. I sit in the front seat and point him in the direction of the hill. Shannon sits silently in the back.

'Up there?' Mr Regan asks, pointing to the ruin at the top

of the hill.

I nod lamely.

'OK. Now, tell me honestly, Freya, was there any drink involved tonight?'

I screw my eyes shut and nod again.

Mr Regan sucks in his breath. 'Right,' he says, parking the car at the foot of the hill. 'You two wait here while I go up.' He shuts the door behind him and we watch as he marches purposefully up the hill.

Shannon shakes my shoulder from the backseat. 'What the hell, Freya? You guys were drinking? Do you realise how serious this is?'

'Izzo,' is all I can manage to say, before welling up again.

Shannon groans. 'No, don't cry. Look, they're going to come down and they're going to be fuming. They'll think we ratted on them. We have to say it was Jackie, that she woke up and checked the room and there was nothing we could do about it. That's the truth anyway.'

Four figures come into view. I hold my breath as they inch closer. *Keep it together, keep it together.* Mr Regan's face is taut with anger and the fear in both Orla and Chloe's faces is illuminated by the car lights. Izzo, meanwhile, looks mildly inconvenienced by the whole affair.

'In. Now,' Mr Regan orders, opening the back door.

Shannon scoots over and they file in obediently.

The few minutes we spend in the car on the way back to the house are unbearably tense, with not even Mr Regan speaking. When we pull into the drive, we are met with a stone-faced Jackie at the front door. She leads us into the kitchen.

'I can't believe you girls,' Mr Regan says. He and Jackie are standing side by side, arms crossed, like two guards. We all stand in a line in front of them, heads down, silent. 'Sneaking out like that, meeting strangers, taking drink. You're a disgrace to Leslie Park. Have you any idea the danger you put yourselves in tonight? And the fright you gave poor Jackie? Anything could've happened to you. Now, tell me, when did you meet these boys?'

'And which ones were they, so I can call their mothers in the morning,' Jackie puts in.

We all instinctively look at Izzo. 'We were just talking one night and one of them asked for my number,' she says innocently. 'It wasn't a big deal.'

'*Isabella*,' Mr Regan says sternly.

Izzo sighs and begins to relay the story. Mr Regan has to interrupt regularly to glean more information from her.

'This one's awfully quiet,' Jackie says, nodding at me. 'What part had you in all this, I wonder?'

My mouth moves to speak, but nothing comes out.

'Freya basically instigated the whole thing,' Izzo says, filling my silence. 'She wanted to see Rory Burns.'

My stomach lurches at the accusation.

'No, she didn't,' Chloe says firmly, looking disgustedly at Izzo. 'Of all of us, Freya wanted to be there the least. *We* made her go.'

The interrogation continues, and once it's been confirmed that Shannon had nothing to do with any of it, she's sent back to her room. Mr Regan calls all of our parents, who all agree to meet at the school tomorrow after pick-up.

'This is just shocking behaviour, girls. Shocking. We'll talk about it more when we're back in Dublin. It's late now though, and we've an early start back in the morning. I want you to apologise to Jackie and go to bed.'

Back in our bedroom, I slip my phone up the sleeve of my jumper and sneak out to the bathroom.

Three missed calls from Mum. I call her back and she answers on the first ring.

'Freya, are you all right? What's going on there? What's happened? Are you OK?'

I press my phone onto my ear, as if it makes Mum closer. 'Freya? Freya?'

I want to respond, but my words have disappeared.

Chapter 22

There's a fleeting moment when I wake the next morning where I don't remember anything. All I am aware of is the heaviness of my bones in my bed, the stickiness of my sleepy eyes. But as my surroundings come into focus, so does my memory. I look around and notice that the others are still asleep. I slip on a pair of socks and tiptoe quietly to the door.

In the dining room, the others are already seated. I take a seat next to Shannon.

OK? she mouths.

I nod. A wordless half-truth, so long as my roommates are still asleep.

I reach for some grapes and listen to Shannon and her roommates as they chatter away. Fatimah is doing impressions of characters from her favourite TV show, to everyone's amusement. It's nice to pretend that everything is normal right now. I'm all too aware that this illusion will shatter the moment my roommates enter the room.

Eventually they file in, all messy hair and puffy-eyes, and take their seats.

'Rat,' Izzo says, glaring at me across the table.

I ignore her and reach for a box of cereal, the only breakfast choice this morning. I fill a small bowl and top it up with oat milk.

'Did you not hear me, rat?'

'Leave her alone,' Shannon says, and the other girls turn to listen.

'This actually has nothing to do with you, psycho. Why were you even there?'

'I saw Freya coming in last night. She wouldn't have gone out in the first place if you hadn't made her.'

'Sorry, are you her babysitter or something? Why can't the rat speak for herself?'

'Iz,' Chloe says softly beside her.

'What? Freya ratted us out and now we're going to get suspended.'

'We are?' Orla says in alarm.

'Eh, what's going on?' Joy asks.

Nobody responds.

I continue my performance of eating a bowl of cereal, even though the flakes are so brittle it feels like I'm eating shards of glass. I try not to think of the ingredients I'm ingesting.

'You're so not getting away with this, Freya,' Izzo says, looking me directly in the eye.

'Get over yourself, Izzo,' Shannon says. 'Mr Regan cornered

140

us both with questions last night. Freya had to tell him the truth.'

'No, she freaked out, then ran away and ratted on us. All I ever tried to do was be nice to you, Freya, but you're honestly such a *weirdo*—'

'She's *autistic*, Izzo, and maybe if you weren't so completely self-absorbed...' Shannon trails off, slowly brings a hand to her mouth. 'Oh my God, Freya, I'm so sorry. I didn't mean to...'

My knuckles blanch as I grip my spoon. Silence descends over the dining room and Izzo's expression is now a mix of disgust and amusement. Her gaze burns through me like antiseptic drenching an open wound. But she is not the only one looking at me. All around me I can feel the eyes of the other girls on me, looking me up and down as if only seeing me for the first time. Even Orla. Heat spreads across my back under their collective gaze, up my arms and legs.

'Well, that explains a lot,' Izzo says, and her laugh is the thing that does it. The thing that finally shatters the snowglobe in my stomach.

I don't remember everything that follows that moment, but I know it involves smashing my cereal bowl on the ground and running out of the dining room screaming.

So much for being normal.

Chapter 23

I haven't touched the sandwich Mum left on my desk for lunch, and the peppermint tea she made me this morning has long since gone cold. My body is surely calling out for sustenance, but my head can't hear it. It's like my brain has been replaced by a scrunched-up piece of paper and nothing is connecting right. All I can do is lie here, replaying the same sorry memory over and over.

She's autistic, Izzo, and maybe if you...

She's autistic, Izzo, and maybe...

She's autistic, Izzo ...

She's autistic.

I squirm at the memory of that morning, my cereal bowl hitting the floor and spraying the other girls with milk and soggy flakes. Running from the room for the bathroom, only to find it occupied, then panicking because I had nowhere to hide.

I curl tightly onto my side and stare at the vintage poster of Steamboat Willie on the wall. My safe place, at last. It's been three days since I got back from Slievanure and I still feel exhausted by it, especially that last morning. I've also developed a cold since coming home, which makes my outside feel as out of order as my inside. At least Mum and Dad have agreed to let me take a few days off school. They were the ones who brought me home from Slievanure in the end, after Mr Regan called them. They saw for themselves how bad I was.

With the bathroom in Jackie's house occupied, the only place I could hide when my surroundings warped into a haunted forest was our bedroom. I ran in and slammed the door after me, but caught something in it by accident. Chloe's arm. She was following after me for some reason. I didn't mean to hurt her; I didn't realise she was there. Everything was so blurry in that moment. Her scream pierced my ears, and I buried my head under my horrible, too-hard pillow to make everything disappear.

Then Jackie came in, ready to give out to me for causing a commotion, but even she seemed alarmed by the sight of me.

'You must be the autistic one,' she said, in that frank, but not unkind way of hers. 'I wasn't sure which one of ye it was. Ah, you poor thing,' she added, rubbing my back in a way that startled me at first. 'You've had a right fright, whatever's happened.'

Jackie stayed with me as Izzo, Chloe and Orla quietly packed their bags and left the room for the last time. I faced the wall so that I wouldn't have to look at them. They didn't even whisper while they were there, and I was grateful to have Jackie nearby.

When the bus came and I wasn't standing outside with the group, Mr Regan came inside to find me. I don't know what the others told him, how they explained everything.

'I don't know what to make of all this,' Jackie said to him. 'I ask her anything and it's half-gibberish, half-cries that comes back. You might give the parents a ring.'

Mum said she'd collect me when Mr Regan called her, that she and Dad would be there within two hours if it was OK with Jackie for me to stay a while longer. Jackie agreed and seemed relieved that Mum's advice was to just leave me alone for a while before checking on me again. I hated them talking like this was some kind of emergency, but I also knew that getting on the bus with the others was impossible.

I shrink at the memory of that morning and remind myself that it's over now, that I'm home and safe again. Home is where I can sketch and play with my dolls and watch the films I like. It's where I don't have to talk if I don't want to or don't feel able. Where I don't have to monitor my face and body and voice. I've been reading Rossa's blog again since coming home, scrolling through his many posts on bees and wildlife in search of anything he's written about autism. I've read about his experience of bullying in primary school and how he mostly likes secondary school. I've read about his younger sister, Emma, who is autistic and non-speaking, and her therapy dog, Biscuit. I feel calm inside when I read his words. They're like a balm over the soreness of everything. A knock at the door rouses me from my thoughts.

'Freya? How're you doing, love?' Mum glances at the untouched sandwich by my bed. 'You need to eat, love. Will you have just a bit of your lunch?'

'I'm not hungry,' I say.

Mum carries the plate to my bed and sits down.

'Here,' she says, ignoring my response and handing me half of the sandwich. 'Toasted, the way you like it.'

I sit up and take it from her, nibble at a corner to please her.

'There you go,' Mum says gently. 'It's important to keep your strength up. How's your temperature?' She places her palm over my forehead. 'Still a bit warm. Just your luck, isn't it? As if you haven't enough on your plate.'

She watches as I eat the sandwich in tiny, reluctant bites. She's undoubtedly taken note of how little I've eaten since returning home.

'Where's Tom?' I ask, my voice hoarse. I haven't spoken much since I got back.

'Watching a match at Brian's. He said he'd be back for dinner. Will we try to sit down together, the four of us?'

I shrug. 'Sure.'

'That girl Shannon called over again. She left this for you.' Mum hands me a small envelope. 'She seems lovely, I must say. And really keen on talking to you.'

I wait until Mum is gone before opening the envelope and unfolding the small note inside.

Dear Freya,

I am so sorry about what happened. My stupid big mouth. I was trying to do the right thing, but I messed up. Please forgive me? I hope you're OK.

Shannon

PS I swear I'm not turning into a stalker; I just don't know how else to reach you. Your address was on that list the school sent home at the start of the year.

PPS I am still so grateful that you felt you could open up to me. I never meant to take that for granted.

I fold the note back inside its envelope.

I don't know if I'm mad at Shannon for what happened. She seems to think I should be, but I can't tell how I actually feel. It's as if my feelings have been blitzed together in a blender and I can't pick them apart. Maybe I'm angry. Maybe I'm sad. Maybe I'm just hungry, or tired. I yawn at that last thought and lower myself back onto my pillow to sleep.

Chapter 24

'Before you say anything, I didn't touch your food,' Tom says as I enter the kitchen the next morning. 'Mum labelled everything and made it very clear that you're being especially *you* these days. Plus, she said she'd buy me take-away if I don't annoy you while I'm home.'

I don't respond, just remove a punnet of blueberries from the fridge and wash them in the kitchen sink. I watch my hands as they shake the excess water from the plastic case and have to remind myself that they belong to me. My body doesn't feel real right now.

'Mum and Dad were telling me about your Irish College escapades. Freya the rebel. Can't say I saw it coming.'

'Me neither,' I say flatly.

'Mum says Orla was involved too, and that Angela went psycho on your principal over it, saying there's no way her angel would ever break the rules. I didn't know you and Orla were even friends anymore.'

Tom had noticed that?

'We're not,' I say coldly. 'We were just roommates.'

Tom hoists himself onto the counter. 'Probably for the best.

Remember the time I accidentally dropped a chicken nugget in her Coke, and it splashed all over her dress? It was at one of your birthday parties. I was trying to catch it in my mouth, but I missed. She told Mum I was bullying her and asked her to make me leave the house. My *own* house.' He shakes his head. 'Drama queen.'

I suppress a small laugh at the memory. Orla and Tom never really got on. Tom was always playing pranks on her and teasing her whenever she was over. The chicken nugget incident was only one in a long line between them.

I prepare a bowl of porridge and bring it to the microwave. When I open the door, I find a spoiled bowl already sitting on the glass plate. 'Tom?'

'Shite,' he says, suddenly remembering he had cooked porridge at all. 'I swear it explodes after a minute.'

'You have to stir it halfway through,' I say, as if for the first time.

'Yeah, yeah,' he says, wiping off lumps on the side of the bowl with kitchen roll. 'So, what are you up to today? Surely you've exhausted the Disney back catalogue by now.'

'*The Lion King Two: Simba's Pride,*' I reply.

'Ew, sequel.'

'It's good for a sequel. I even prefer some of the songs in it to the original.'

'Better than *Hakuna Matata*? Please.'

'Watch it and see for yourself.'

Tom exhales dramatically. 'Fine. It's not like I have anything else to do today anyway. We're getting proper snacks for it though. None of those weird nut bars you pretend to like.'

I look at him suspiciously.

'Not that I've ever tried them. I'd obviously never defy your labels.' He blushes and turns towards the sink to scrub his porridge bowl. When his back is turned, I smile.

Tom drives us to Tesco and we scour the sweet aisle together.

'These are great,' he says, picking up a bag of jellybeans with a gooey centre that looks like washing up liquid. 'You can get two bags for a pound in the Sainsbury's opposite my flat. We probably get through about four bags a week.' He pulls two bags from the rack and drops them into the basket, then wanders off in search of biscuits.

I follow him from aisle to aisle, listening as he talks to himself aloud and tries to decide what to buy. I try not to let it show, but I feel uneasy surrounded by so much junk food, like I need to scrub myself clean just looking at it. I wander back to the front of the shop and wait for Tom at the self-checkout. I distract myself by scrolling through Rossa's Instagram, grateful for the many pictures of honeybees at work that squash down thoughts of refined sugar.

Did you know that, in her entire lifetime, a honeybee produces approximately one twelfth of a teaspoon of honey? If you eat honey, please take a moment to appreciate the work the honeybee has done to bring it to you!

'Can you believe these are only a euro?' Tom says, triumphant as he holds up a bag of discounted Halloween sweets.

I slip my phone into my pocket, thoughts of honeybees flying out of my head as memories of Irish College flood in. I usually loved Halloween, but this year had been horrible. Memories of sneaking out to the castle – of Izzo, Burns, the car, the hill – loop around and around in my head. Why couldn't I just have stayed home this Halloween, dressed up as Hei Hei and watched *Hocus Pocus* with Mum instead?

Tom empties the various treats he's bought into bowls and sets them on the coffee table in the front room.

'Right. *Simba's Pride.* I'll try to keep an open mind.'

'You won't be disappointed,' I say.

'Yeah, yeah. Here,' he says, and passes a bowl of jellybeans to me.

I shake my head.

Tom frowns. 'Seriously? You've only had porridge today, and that was hours ago.'

'Porridge is filling!' I say innocently.

'Freya. Come on.'

'What?' I act like I'm clueless.

'They're worried about you, you know.'

I scoff dramatically, as if what he's saying is ridiculous, even though it isn't. 'I just don't want any of those sweets. They look gross. Can you play the film now please?'

'Fine,' Tom says, putting the bowl back on the coffee table.

We don't talk during the film, and instead of watching and listening to the songs I love, I'm thinking about Tom and how annoying I forgot he is. Since he left for college, I haven't had to label my food or worry about anyone criticising what I eat. Now, after less than a day together, he's right back to being a nosy know-it-all. Today is the first time in months I've seen my brother, and already I'm counting down the days until he's gone again.

Chapter 25

Food was the last topic Elaine brought up during my assessment last summer. By now, she had asked me about school, home, childhood and friendships. I'd had to dig deep in my memory to answer some of her questions, sometimes unearthing unpleasant memories in the process. It was tiring, even with all the breaks Elaine gave me. Now we were going to talk about food, a conversation that would drain me completely.

'Can you remember when you first began restricting?' Elaine asked.

'Before Christmas,' I admitted. 'Around October or November, I think.'

'And can you remember how it began?'

I tried to sound casual. 'I just wanted to be healthier.'

Elaine nodded sympathetically. 'So you decided to cut back on certain things – certain ingredients – and then you cut out other things gradually. Is that right?'

I crossed my ankles and squeezed my feet as tightly as I could in my shoes. 'Yeah.'

'And did you feel healthier?'

I met Elaine's eye and instantly felt my resolve crumble.

'It's OK, Freya,' she said patiently. 'Take your time.'

I took a tissue from the box beside me and blew my nose.

'I just wanted to fix my brain,' I said, my voice small and cracked. 'It's broken somehow. It doesn't work like other people's.'

'What makes you think that?' Elaine asked, her voice neutral as ever.

'Because I'm slow and stupid and I always get things wrong, no matter how hard I try. But then I read an article in a magazine at the dentist one day about the food you have to eat for a healthy brain, and I thought…' I brought my heels to the edge of my chair and buried my face behind my knees.

'Take your time, Freya.'

I sniffed loudly and wiped my nose again. 'It said that things like berries and nuts and grains make your brain healthy, so that's what I ate. I stopped eating bad food and only ate the stuff the article said to. I thought it would fix my brain and make me normal. I thought it would clean all the badness and stupidness and wrongness away.' I pressed my hands into the sides of my legs as Elaine considered everything I'd said, willing myself not to go full Snow White in front of her.

'I understand,' Elaine said, her voice warmer than it had been all morning. 'I really do. I understand.'

Elaine explained that the article had been misleading, that

she thought I had taken it too literally, but that that wasn't my fault. She told me there was nothing wrong with my brain, and that I struggled with things for other reasons, none of which were wrong or my fault. I got annoyed with her then, shaking my head and telling her she was wrong, that she didn't understand. I started to really cry then, the heaving, gasping, messy kind that feels impossible to talk through and more impossible to stop. Elaine slid a pen and paper across the coffee table between us.

'Write it down,' she said. 'It might be easier. Write it all down until you feel you've said everything.'

I clicked the top of the pen and set the tip against the blank sheet of paper. Almost immediately, the words began to pour.

You don't know what it's like being stupid. And I don't just mean school stupid, I mean human stupid. You don't know what it's like to have to practise everything you want to say before you say it, in case you say the wrong thing or use the wrong tone of voice. You don't know what it's like to lose track of a conversation because the other person's words are coming too fast and your brain can't catch everything or start panicking in a group because everyone is talking, and you don't know how to include yourself. All the things other people do without thinking, I have to think about. I have to watch and listen and copy everything around me if I want to seem normal. It's like I'm an actor and every day I have to learn a new script and play a part at the same time. It's exhausting. Pre-

tending to be a normal person when you're actually some kind of broken-brained alien is exhausting.

The page was dotted with damp circles where my tears had landed, and my hand ached from gripping the pen so tightly. I felt light afterwards though, like my body had purged every last thought and there was nothing left inside of me. In a way, there wasn't. Elaine had now learned everything about me, scraped the inside of my mind clean. There was nothing more to say.

Some Thoughts About Turtles

I've been reading a lot about turtles and tortoises recently, after finding a book on testudines in my local library. I find them fascinating creatures to read about and enjoy learning interesting facts about them. Something I had never considered about testudines before is the fact that their shells are part of their skeletons, not simply attached to them. Unlike hermit crabs, for example, who frequently abandon their old shells and search for new ones as they grow, testudines cannot be separated from their shells.

This got me thinking about autism. As many of you know, I prefer to describe myself as an autistic person, rather than a person with autism. In fact, many people in the autistic community feel the same way. I think this is because, like a turtle and its shell, autistic people can't be separated from autism. It isn't an add-on part of our identity; it's an inherent part of who we are that shapes how we perceive and process the world around us. Many of us take pride in that fact, even though living in a world that doesn't always understand our differences and needs can be challenging.

Describing myself as an autistic person rather than a person with autism doesn't mean that I'm only defined by autism, but recognises that autism is a central part of my identity. It's for that same reason that I describe myself as Irish, rather than a person with Irishness. It doesn't take away from the fact that I'm also a beekeeper, a blogger, a brother, and a dozen other things. Saying I'm autistic is simply a way of acknowledging that autism is a core part of who I am, just like a shell is to a turtle. It's a neutral fact about me, but also one I happen to be very proud of!

Chapter 26

'All set for today?' Mum asks me in the kitchen.

'Yeah,' I lie.

Ideally, I would never return to school, but I know there's no point in trying to fight the inevitable.

'Well, just get through the first few days, and you can have a nice, quiet weekend.' Mum clears her throat then. 'And you'll make sure to eat your lunch, won't you?' She looks at me imploringly.

'Yes,' I say irritably. I knew she'd been keeping tabs on my eating. 'I always do.'

'I know, love. It's just… I'm worried that you've been pushing food away since you got back. Dad and I have both noticed, and Tom mentioned it too, before he left.'

'I'm fine,' I say.

'We just don't want you slipping into old habits again. It's a hard thing to recover from. I think we all need to remember that.'

I know that by 'thing' she means 'eating disorder'. What she doesn't know is that it's not as simple as just sticking to my meal plan. She doesn't know about the voices I wrestle against every time I bring food to my lips, especially ones I had cut out for months. These voices taunted me when I ate, told me that I was losing control and waving goodbye to any chance of being normal. They had gotten louder since I came back from Irish College, but my family didn't appreciate that. They could only see what I didn't eat, never what I did, despite the voices telling me not to.

The school is practically empty when I arrive, save for a few teachers dashing about with stacks of photocopying and steaming mugs of bitter-smelling coffee. In the next hour these same quiet corridors will be teeming with hundreds of girls in identical woollen jumpers, all talking and laughing and creating a wall of noise around them. I savour this small pocket of silence as I make my way up to Ms Connolly.

'Freya,' Ms Connolly says, alerted by the creak of the door. 'Thanks for coming in early. Happy to be back?'

'Yeah,' I say, unconvincingly.

'Because we can talk about it if you're not.'

'I'm OK.'

'Good. And how were your few days at home? Feeling better?'

I drop my gaze into my lap. 'Mm.'

'Look, Freya, I know that you were pressured to take part

in the incident at Slievanure. Chloe spoke to me about it and explained things, and Mr Regan expressed his view on the matter too. All things considered, it wouldn't have been right to suspend you.'

I look up at her. 'Suspend me?'

'Well, yes. The others have been absent the last few days too on suspension. Consumption of alcohol at school-organised events is against school policy. The Board was adamant that there'd be consequences for what happened.'

I feel dizzy taking in this information. 'My roommates got suspended?'

Ms Connolly nods. 'Sorry, I thought your parents would have told you. They were suspended for three days, but are all back now. Are you all right, Freya?'

I realise I'm breathing quickly. 'I… I just didn't know that.'

And I hope this doesn't mean I'm in even more trouble with them.

'I'm sure your parents just didn't want to worry you during your time at home. You've had a lot on your mind this week, haven't you? A lot to *process*.'

The word is delicate on her tongue, carefully plucked, I suspect, from one of the pamphlets I've noticed peeking out from under the piles of paperwork on her desk. *Supporting Students On the Spectrum. Understanding Students With Autism.* The kind of well-meaning literature so often accompanied by images of children's shadows in empty playgrounds and puzzle pieces in disarray. We are the unreachable, these images seem to suggest, even though we're right here.

I nod on cue.

'Well, we can ease you back gently into school life. You can continue to take your lunch in the library if that helps, and you can call into me whenever you need to. And why don't we get started on study skills soon, hm? You might find it useful having something to focus on. Christmas exams will come around before you know it.'

'Yes, Ms Connolly.'

As I stand to take my leave, my vision blurs momentarily and I grip the top of my chair for balance. Ms Connolly doesn't seem to notice. I wander as casually as possible out of her office, black stars twinkling in the corners of my eyes as I go.

Chapter 27

If I've ever felt self-conscious about having greasy hair in school, or paranoid after forgetting to put on deodorant, today is worse than both of those things combined. I'd take looking like I got caught in the rain because I forgot to shower or stinking of B.O. any day over how I feel today. I've rushed in and out of my classes all morning, trying to avoid everyone's gaze, especially Orla, Chloe and Izzo's, and tried my best to listen to my teachers for fear of being called out and casting an even bigger spotlight over myself. At small break, I hid in the third-floor toilets, my face planted into my hands as I tried to keep my breathing steady.

When the bell finally rings for lunch, I feel my body melt a little, knowing the library will give me some refuge from this horrible day.

I've just taken out my lunch when Shannon appears.

'Freya,' she says, as if it's been years and not days. 'You're back.' Her smile is wide and hopeful. Then she looks down at her feet, like a guilty dog. 'Did you get my note?'

'Yeah.'

'I'm so sorry if I was invading your space, I just wanted to apologise. About everything. I was such an idiot saying that in front of everyone. You probably think I'm a total bitch, and I honestly get it if you do. I've been thinking so much about everything and if I could go back and change things, I would, but obviously I can't and now I'm wondering what I can do to make it better. If I even *can* make it better.'

I want to hold up my hands to stop any more of her words from bombarding me. My brain can only process teaspoons at a time right now, and here Shannon is throwing buckets' worth at me.

'Freya,' she says again. 'I really am so sorry. I totally get why you're giving me the silent treatment. If there's anything I can do...'

The silent treatment. It almost makes me laugh. Like I'm choosing not to talk much these days, and not that my brain doesn't know how to. I don't know what to say to Shannon right now and am relieved when Ms Horgan approaches us.

'Girls,' she says excitedly. 'Big news. Helena Carmody, the Minister for Education, is going to officially open the new library for us in a few weeks' time.' She pauses for reaction, but neither Shannon nor I say anything. 'I was thinking, wouldn't it be great if the Library Committee from each year made a display for her visit. Like a little exhibition. What do you think?'

Shannon looks at me blankly. 'Ehh, sounds cool? What kind of display would we have to make?'

'Something based on our books, I suppose, so that we can show what an inspiring facility the library is. There'll be some press at the opening too. The *Times* is going to include the story in a broader piece about school library funding. So something that's eye-catching for the camera!'

Ms Horgan floats back to her piles of books on the far end of the room.

'Any ideas?' Shannon says.

I shake my head.

Shannon starts rummaging in a nearby box. 'Ooh, what about something like this?' She holds up a collection of fairy tales. 'We could do a display on Irish fairies, like the ones we learned about on the walk with P.J.'

'No,' I say firmly. There's no way I'm willingly doing a project on changelings.

'These illustrations are so cool and creepy,' Shannon says, absorbed by the book in her hands. 'And look at the picture of the author. She looks like a fairy queen!'

I clock the author's name, Sinéad de Valera, and another idea comes to me.

'We could do an exhibition on Irish women writers,' I say. 'We could recreate the poster opposite Ms Connolly's office that's all male writers, and make one that's all women.' I have no idea where this idea has come from, but it's remarkably fully formed. More importantly, Shannon is now clapping her fingertips and grinning.

'Oh my God,' she says. 'I have no idea what poster you're talking about, but that sounds *amazing*! I'm in.'

I breathe a sigh of relief. No changelings.

The library door swings open and Chloe wanders in. 'Hey, Freya,' she says shyly.

'Hi,' I say, feeling my fingers start to twitch. Chloe is *here*? Of all the confrontations I feared happening today, this was by far the worst. How could I ever explain myself to Chloe or expect her to forgive me for catching her arm in a door?

'How're you feeling?' she asks. She doesn't look angry at me. She looks… concerned?

'I'm fine,' I say. 'How are you?' The question is more of a reflex.

'Good. Weird to be back, isn't it? Honestly, being suspended was kind of nice.'

I feel my eyebrows lift a fraction. Did they think I got suspended too?

'At least I got some extra ukulele practice out of all of this,' Chloe says. 'What did you get up to?'

I try to formulate a response in my head, but realise I can't do small talk today. 'I'm sorry about your arm,' I say, getting it over with. 'I didn't mean to…'

She shakes her head. 'It's fine. You didn't know I was there. I didn't mean to scare you, I just wanted to see if I could help.'

'Help?'

'Well, you were having a meltdown, right? My cousin has them and I know they're really scary for him. My aunts always try to gauge if he needs somebody with him before giving him space. I was trying to follow their lead, but I guess I got it wrong. Not that I'm comparing you to my cousin or anything; I know autistic people are all different. I just recognised a couple of signs from when he gets overwhelmed.'

I'm stunned by how frankly Chloe talks about autism and meltdowns, almost like they're normal. 'Thanks,' I say quietly.

She smiles. 'Sure. I just wanted to clear the air.' She looks around. 'This place is so weird. It's like a little hovel in the middle of the school. It doesn't even have windows.'

'We like it,' Shannon says. 'Hovel sweet hovel, and all that. The lack of natural daylight probably isn't great though. The new library will be like a palace compared to this.'

It's only as she says it that I realise I will miss this hovel when it's gone.

I'm walking home from school when I hear my name being called behind me. I turn around and see Izzo and Orla walking towards me. *Oh God.* I shouldn't have thought I'd gotten away without seeing them today.

'Hey, Freya!' Izzo says, her voice high and sweet. 'How *are* you?'

'Fine,' I say on cue, my gaze fixed on the pavement below me.

'Aw, that's good. So weird being back, isn't it? I still can't believe they suspended us. So dramatic.' She rolls her eyes. 'Still, I guess it's only fair that we *all* got punished. It was all of our fault really.'

I don't say anything.

'By the way, Freya,' Izzo continues, 'I'm so sorry, I never realised you were, you know... *challenged*?' She pretends to whisper the word. 'I guess it kind of makes sense, though. I don't mean that in a bad way or anything! I just mean, like, it's not that surprising when you think about it, you know?'

I look up to find her smiling coldly at me. Orla is silent beside her.

'Anyway, we're heading to Dundrum. We're shopping for...' Orla nudges her forcefully in the arm.

Izzo smirks. 'Never mind. So nice to see you again, Freya,' she says as she and Orla walk off. 'Look after yourself.' She says the words slowly, like English isn't my first language.

I spend the afternoon on my bedroom floor, surrounded by sketches, pencil parings flitted around the carpet like confetti. Losing myself in ideas for the library project is the only thing that takes my mind off school. I'm so engrossed by my frantic efforts that I don't hear Mum opening my bedroom door.

'You didn't eat your lunch today,' she says, looking down at me. 'It's still there in your bag, untouched.'

'I didn't have time,' I say, taken aback by this confrontation. 'I had to do stuff for the Library Committee at lunch.'

'Freya.' Mum is serious. 'You promised me.'

'I'm not lying,' I say, feeling my cheeks warm.

'Do you realise what'll happen if you fall back into this pattern again?' Mum says, not listening to me. 'We'll have to take you back to the hospital, and it'll be back to square one all over again. Is that what you want?'

What I want? I feel myself getting defensive. 'I already told you; I didn't have time to eat my lunch today. Ms Horgan told us we had to do a project, and then Shannon and I were–'

'No,' Mum says. 'I'm sick to my teeth of these excuses, Freya, and I can't keep giving into them. You were too tired to eat when you came home, then you were too sick. So long as you're battling this problem, you'll always find an excuse not to eat. I can't watch you fall off track again. I won't let you. Now, come on, your dinner's ready.'

She steps aside as if expecting me to follow her to the kitchen. She thinks she's right about everything.

'I'm not lying,' I say again, staring at her intently. 'And even when I didn't want to eat all those times, I still did. I just didn't have time today.'

Mum's jaw is tight. 'Right, well, you have plenty of time

now. Come on.' I can't stand this tone. She doesn't believe me.

'I'm not lying,' I say again.

'You've made that very clear, Freya. Now, come on. Please.'

'No,' I say. 'I'm not going when you don't believe me.'

'That's really not the point,' Mum says. 'Your dinner's getting cold.'

She's not listening to me. Why isn't she listening? 'No,' I say again, my heart knocking against my chest.

'Freya, get up.'

'NO,' I shout at her. 'Stop telling me what to do!'

'Freya!' she snaps. 'Get up this minute and come down for your dinner. I won't tell you again.'

I feel my top lip twitch as I look into her hard, unblinking eyes. Then, I scream. A scream so loud it burns my throat and makes my temples throb. 'Get out! Get out, get out, get out, GET OUT!' I scoop up my sketches, scrunch them up and fling them at her. 'GET. OUT.'

'Freya!'

'No! I hate you! I hate you more than anyone in the entire world. You always pretend you're on my side, but you don't care about me. I didn't want to go to school today, but you made me. Now you won't believe me even though I'm telling you the truth, and you're bossing me around like I'm a little kid. I hate you!'

I collapse over myself then, press my face into the carpet, slap my palms on the ground as images of Izzo, Orla, Irish College,

Tom, school and everything else flash through my mind. 'I hate you,' I repeat through my tears. 'I hate you. I hate you.' I lie there for a few minutes, sniffing and shuddering. When I look up again, Mum is gone.

Please Don't Call Me 'High-Functioning'

When I was identified as autistic at the age of seven, our family doctor assured my mam that I would do OK in life because I was 'high-functioning'. This meant that I could talk like non-autistic people, go to school with non-autistic people and appear, in many ways, like non-autistic people. At worst, being 'high-functioning' simply meant I had some challenges with social interaction and sensory processing and was 'rigid' in my routines and interests. It meant people often using the movie *Rain Man* as a point of reference to make sense of me. It wasn't until my little sister, Emma, was born that I really started to resent the term.

Emma is six, autistic, and predominantly non-speaking. She has a few mouth words, but mostly she gestures or makes noises when she's communicating with us. Because of her lack of speech, people make assumptions about Emma's ability and intelligence. They assume that she is unthinking, unhearing, and unfeeling. They overlook the things she can do, like sing and colour and count, and focus on what she can't. They use terms like 'low-functioning' to describe her.

Just because Emma doesn't communicate with words (we don't know if she ever will), it doesn't mean that she is 'low-functioning'. Similarly, just because I am writing this blog right now, it doesn't mean that I am 'high-functioning'. We both have our challenges and support needs, and there is a lot beneath the surface for both of us that other people can't see. My needs shouldn't be overlooked or dismissed because I 'pass as normal' in some people's eyes, and Emma's potential shouldn't be underestimated simply because she communicates differently to most other people. Functioning labels are reductive and hurt autistic people. Worst of all though, they create a harmful divide in our community. I don't think of myself as better than 'other' autistic people simply because I am more independent than them in some ways. I don't think it is a badge of honour to be in another category to anyone else, simply because I can speak, for example, or don't have a learning disability. I proudly stand alongside Emma and every other autistic person, not separate from them. Autistic people may be different in some ways, but we are still all part of the same community.

Chapter 28

'These are cool,' Shannon says, looking through the selection of drawings I've brought in. I had to smooth them out after scrunching them up yesterday and told her they got crumpled in my school bag. 'Whoa, what's going on in this one? Freaky.'

She holds up a rough sketch of a goblin-like creature in a bassinet. 'Nothing,' I say quickly, taking my drawing of a changeling from her. It must have slipped in by mistake when I was packing my bag for school.

'Well, these are all awesome. I'll keep researching more writers to include. We should have twelve soon, just like the original poster. I'm loving the ones I've got so far, by the way. If I wasn't sure before that I wanted to be a writer, I'm absolutely certain now. These women are all so cool and interesting. Like, this one woman, Ella Young, wrote Celtic myths for children and lectured about fairy tales in a university in California while wearing purple robes. Apparently, they detained her at Ellis Island because she kept talking about fairies and elves! Oh, and some people say she was a lesbian and was in love with Maud Gonne. You know, the woman Yeats relentlessly nice-guyed for years before asking her daughter to marry him. What a creep! Are you OK? You're really quiet today.'

'I was sketching pretty late,' I say, which isn't a lie.

I stayed up until Mum and Dad went to bed, so that I could go to the kitchen without having to deal with either of them. I was starving by then, but I couldn't face Mum. I don't know how I might have reacted if she or Dad brought up food again.

'Is that all?' Shannon says.

'Hm?'

She looks sheepish. 'Well, I realise we never really talked about Irish College again. Are we OK?'

I had almost forgotten about that. 'It's fine,' I say.

'You're sure?'

'Yeah.'

'You're *sure* you're sure?'

'Yeah.' I try to sound more convincing this time.

Shannon smiles. 'Phew. I thought maybe you were still...' She shrugs. 'I'm really sorry again.'

'I'm sorry too,' I say.

'Huh? For what?'

'For what I said in the bathroom that time, about you following me. It was really mean.'

Amidst everything else that's been clogging my brain for the last few days is the memory of Shannon trying to help me in the bathroom in Slievanure and me being rude to her.

I wasn't sure how I felt about it until the same feeling of sea-sickness consumed me yesterday after my fight with Mum. I think it was guilt.

'Thanks,' Shannon says, and I feel lighter already. One less previously unidentified emotion disentangled from the knot inside me. 'I've been reading a little about autism, by the way,' she says then. 'I realised when you said it to me that I had no idea what it actually was. Like, I remember this boy in my primary school who used to flap his hands a lot, but I never knew what that was about. It's stimming, right? Autistic people do it to manage their feelings?'

I instinctively dig my fingertips into my palms as she speaks.

'And then I read that girls can be really good at masking autism, and that made sense to me because Chloe said something similar on the bus home.'

The thought of everyone discussing what happened on the bus makes my stomach clench. Who was there for that? Were Izzo and Orla? Were Shannon's roommates? The thought sparks a question.

'Why were you in our house in Irish College?'

Shannon begins leafing through a book on her desk distractedly. 'Oh, that. Yeah, mildly embarrassing, but I guess I don't really have any friends in school. I kind of knew Fatimah in First Year so I asked if I could stay with her. It worked out pretty well in the end. Those girls are all really nice and funny.'

'How come you don't spend more time with them now? Like at lunchtime?'

Shannon shrugs. 'This hovel kind of has a place in my heart.'

I smile. I'm glad Shannon was in our house in Irish College.

Chapter 29

'Freya, are you with me?' Ms Connolly says.

'Hm?'

'I said I want you to have a read through these different learning styles and tell me which one you think describes you best.' She looks down at the doodle of a fish on my worksheet. 'I have my own suspicions, but let's see how you get on.'

The fish is Dory from *Finding Nemo*. I found myself doodling her while Ms Connolly was explaining the difference between short- and long-term memory. I can't remember what she said it is, but our first study-skills session is going well otherwise.

I glance at the statements and put a tick in the box I think sounds most like me.

When I hear the word cat I... picture a cat in my mind

I prefer when teachers... write information on the white board

When I take a test... I picture the answers as they appeared in my notes or textbook

I slide the worksheet over to Ms Connolly when I'm finished.

'A visual learner,' she says in a tone that suggests she is not surprised at all. 'A very creative learning style. It's something we can keep in mind when we're putting your study timetable together. You might like something that's colour-coded or has images. Oh, I found this in one of the supply cupboards and thought you might find it useful.' She places a clock on her desk. 'It's a visual timer. The clock face changes colour as time passes, so it's easier to manage time. We had a student with ADHD a few years ago who loved it. Would you like to try using it for home study?'

'OK,' I say, taking the clock to inspect.

'Great. Now, I'd like us to try another reading comprehension before you go. I found an article online I thought you might like. I wrote out a few questions to go with it.'

She hands me a print-out and I'm surprised to see a picture of Rossa staring back at me. *Teen With Autism Creates Galway's First Bee-Friendly Bus Stop*, the headline reads.

'I know him,' I say, taking in the picture of Rossa standing in front of a bus stop grinning. 'Well, I read his blog sometimes.'

'Isn't it wonderful? I had a look at it myself after finding this article. Fantastic young man and a great role model. Have you found his blog helpful?'

I nod. I had found Rossa's blog helpful, especially since returning home from Irish College. When I struggled to put things into words, his ability to do it so well made me feel calm.

'That's great. I shared it with one of the First Years too. She's autistic, like you. Diagnosed in primary school, but still finding her feet with it, I think.'

I feel my cheeks go warm. Ms Connolly means the girl Izzo and Orla laughed at in Irish College and called weird.

'Let's see what Rossa has to say about bees then, shall we?' Ms Connolly says. 'Have a read through the piece yourself and we'll try the questions at the end together. Remember to keep an eye out for *keywords;* names, dates, locations and that. These are what'll help you answer the questions more efficiently in an exam. You can use a highlighter if it's helpful.'

I'm a few minutes late leaving Ms Connolly's office and rushing to my next class when I hear the distinctive clip-clop of teachers' heels behind me. I grip the straps of my school bag in anticipation of getting told off for being late, when Ms Kavanagh and another teacher sashay past. Ms Kavanagh locks eyes with me, but doesn't say anything.

'Is she the one? You wouldn't know it looking at her, would you?' the other teacher says as they walk down the corridor.

Ms Kavanagh sucks her teeth. 'Sure, half of them are diagnosed with something these days. You'd be hard pressed to keep up.'

They snigger and disappear around the corner.

'How did the session with Ms Connolly go today, Freya?' Dad asks at the dinner table. He's taken charge of making small talk since Mum and I still are barely speaking.

'Fine,' I say, spooning a portion of roasted vegetables onto my plate. I can feel Mum's eyes on me the whole time. 'She says I'm a visual learner. It's why I like doodling, apparently.'

Dad laughs. 'I'd well believe that. Can't leave a sheet of paper down in this house without finding it tattooed in pen later.'

'We read an article about an autistic boy called Rossa,' I say, in an attempt to patch over the memory of the incident with Ms Kavanagh. 'He created the first bee-friendly bus stop in his town by planting flowers on top of the roof. Now the County Council is going to plant them everywhere. He also has a blog and writes a lot about autism. I read it sometimes.'

Dad glances at Mum to determine how to react. I've never dropped the A-word so casually in conversation before.

'That's great,' Dad ventures. 'Sounds like a bright lad.'

'Yeah, he's really smart. And he knows *so* much about bees. Like, about *hundreds* of species of them. It's impressive.'

I take the last bites of my dinner and excuse myself to finish my drawing of Edna O'Brien in my room.

In the hall, I hear Mum talking to Dad. 'Well, that was… positive. Do you think she's turning a corner maybe?'

'She might be,' Dad says.

A small part of me wonders the same thing.

Chapter 30

I'm walking home from the LUAS stop, my new Belle doll safely stashed in my school bag, when I hear my name being called through my headphones. I pause my Disney playlist and am surprised to see Angela, Orla's mum. She ambles over to me, two large shopping bags straining under her arms.

'I thought it was you, Freya,' she says, catching her breath. 'Are you well, love? You're up and about very early for a Saturday. Orla was still snoring away when I left the house this morning.' She rolls her eyes theatrically, even though it seems perfectly reasonable that Orla would still be asleep at nine o'clock on a Saturday morning.

'I had to buy a present for my cousin,' I lie. It's the first time I've used my lie about the magazines, and I'm glad I had the foresight to come up with it.

'Very good. I'm just getting a head start on the Christmas shopping myself,' Angela says, holding up the bulging shopping bags. 'I swear it comes around earlier every year.' Her eyes are fixed on me and I can sense she has more to say. Then: 'Orla mentioned…' She pulls in her lips as she considers her next words. 'Well, she mentioned something about you having *autism.'* She makes a face as if to say, *Isn't that mad?* 'I told her she must have misheard, that maybe someone said you were *artistic…'* She looks at me for clarification.

'It's true,' I say quietly, as if I've just confessed to a petty crime.

Angela's head tilts a fraction. 'Well, now, that's very surprising, isn't it? I would have thought you were, well, normal. A bit quiet maybe, but definitely normal.' She shakes her head then, as if she can't believe it. 'Anyway, you'd never know it, looking at you. You hide it very well. And you're getting prettier every day, God bless you.'

I smile blandly.

'Come here, are you all right after the trip? Poor Orla was devastated by the whole thing. They'd some neck suspending you all, hadn't they? A bit of an overreaction, if you ask me.' She sighs. 'I think it was all that Izzo one's doing. You and Orla just got caught up in her scheme, you poor things. Anyway, I won't keep you any longer, Freya. Give my best to your mum and dad, won't you?'

I nod politely and watch as she toddles off with her shopping bags, trying not to let my alarm at Orla and Angela discussing my brain register on my face.

In my room, I unpack my new Belle doll with shaky hands. I

try to distract myself by smoothing the ruffles on her yellow gown, but other people's voices twist through my head like a corkscrew and I can't concentrate.

I would have thought you were, well, normal.

I never realised you were, you know... challenged?

Sure, half of them are diagnosed with something these days.

You hide it very well.

I try to push them away, but they stay stuck on a loop in my mind.

'Freya?' Mum calls up the stairs. 'Is that you? Are you coming down for your breakfast?'

Of course she noticed that I left this morning without eating.

'In a minute!' I call back. I don't want to fight her again, but I need a moment to myself.

Hot emotion bubbles inside me as the voices churn over in my head. It seems that everyone has something to say about autism, some opinion. Everyone thinks they're right, but nobody really understands. Nobody tries to understand. They hear a word and make assumptions and I have no say in anything. I hate it. I hate being misunderstood. How can a diagnosis be a good thing when nobody understands what it means? Whatever is bubbling inside me is getting louder, like a boiling kettle.

'Freya?' Mum calls again.

'In a minute!' I shout back.

I wish I was invisible. I don't want people making comments about me or thinking that they know me better than I know myself.

I would have thought you were, well, normal.

I never realised you were, you know… challenged?

Sure, half of them are diagnosed with something these days.

You hide it very well.

I screw my eyes shut and press my palms over my eyes, but the voices keep repeating and repeating and…

'Freya?' Mum calls again.

With that, I pick up my new Belle doll and fire her against the wall. I clap a hand over my mouth as her porcelain head cracks in two and falls away from the rest of her body. Half of her hollow head looks up at me from the carpet, while the other half faces the ceiling. Tears blur my vision as I sit staring at her.

Education should be for everyone, not just some

School has never been easy for me, but with support from my teachers and SNAs over the years, it has been mostly manageable. I've always been in a mainstream class, which is often a stressful environment because there are so many other students and it's usually loud and busy. I found it much harder to cope in this kind of setting when I was younger. I was often disruptive without realising it and not very good at following rules. I remember getting into trouble a lot, even though I was actually pretty shy. But then in First Class, my teacher, Mrs. Lennon, saw things from a different angle. She could see that I was struggling in different ways and talked to my mam about it. That conversation eventually led to me getting diagnosed with something called Asperger's Syndrome. (Asperger's is no longer an official diagnosis, and nowadays people are diagnosed with autism instead).

School got better for me after that point because I had more support. My teachers now knew that I needed breaks during the day to help me regulate and stay calm. They knew things like fire drills were incredibly stressful and painful for me and let me wear ear defenders when I needed them. They knew that I needed more time to do my work in class because I find it hard to organise myself. It didn't make everything suddenly perfect, but there's no question that being identified as autistic changed my school experience for the better. I wish it was the same for all autistic people.

Next year, my little sister, Emma, is supposed to be starting school, but she hasn't got a place anywhere. Mam thinks that a mainstream class would be too challenging for her and that an autism class would be more appropriate, and so does Emma psychologist. Autism classes are much smaller (they only have six students, whereas mainstream classes sometimes have more than thirty), so teachers can give students a lot more individual support and attention. The problem is, there aren't enough autism classes in Ireland for children like Emma, and there are none in our area. This means that Emma will have to get home tutoring until we can find an appropriate place for her in a school. It means that my mam will have to continue knocking on school doors all around the county and writing emails to the government long after other children Emma's age have gotten a start on their education.

Emma has a right to go to school just like everyone else, but because she needs more support than most other children, she is being left out and left behind. The worst thing is, there are hundreds of other autistic kids and teenagers in the same boat as Emma. This is a serious civil rights issue that more people in Ireland need to care about, whether they're directly impacted by it or not. Mam says trying to talk to politicians is like talking to a brick wall sometimes, but if enough of us try, maybe we can break that wall down and make change happen. That's what Emma deserves, after all. It's what every autistic person in Ireland deserves.

Chapter 31

'm working on a sketch of Maeve Binchy, trying to capture the warmth of her smile, when my phone vibrates beside me. I assume it's Shannon with another idea for our display and start when I see that it's a message from Orla.

Hey, wanna come over for a movie tomo?

I set my phone down again and gaze at the message in wonder, as if it's the first message I've ever been sent. I tap out of it and then open it up again, just to make sure it's really there. Then I scroll up through my conversation history with Orla, and wince at our last messages to each other.

Me, in September: **Do you want to walk to school together on Monday?? Xxx**

Me, the next day: **Hey! Want to walk to school together tomorrow? Xxx**

Me, the day after that: **I can call to you on the way to school tomorrow, if you want xx**

Me, that evening: **Hey are u ok??**

Orla, finally: **Oops, sorry didn't see ur messages until now :/**

Since smashing my Belle doll last week, I've hardly talked to anyone besides Shannon, and that's mostly been in the context of our project. I don't know how I'd be coping without the project to bury myself under completely. Mum is still monitoring my eating and I feel tired on Dad's behalf as he tries to disguise the tension in the house with endless small talk. It's been a mostly horrible time, but now, out of the blue, I've received a message from Orla asking to hang out.

I had thought about Orla a lot since Irish College. I'd thought about her getting suspended and how upset Angela said she'd been. Was what Angela said true, about Orla feeling pressured into sneaking out by Izzo like I had been? Has Orla been feeling as blurry and muddled up as I have since we got back? It's been over a year since she invited me to her house for a movie. After everything that happened, does she want us to be friends again? As I'm thinking about how to reply to her message, another thought hits me. Today is Orla's *birthday*. I double check the date on my phone to be sure. Yes! How had I not remembered? My phone feels suddenly heavy in my hand. Orla was reaching out to *me* on *her* birthday. This has to mean something.

I begin typing *happy birthday,* but it doesn't feel right. I usually made a much bigger effort than this. I usually made a card and hand-delivered it to her house in the morning. I always got her a present. I look down at my pencils and sketchbook. It wasn't too late to make her a card and call over to her house. She couldn't get annoyed with me for giving her a card, could she? Maybe she was expecting it. I doubt Izzo would make her a personalised birthday card. I pull a sheet from my sketch-pad, fold it neatly in half and begin sketching some of Orla's favourite things: sweets, make-up brands, shoes, movies. Well, things that were definitely her favourite things once. I'm not entirely sure what her favourite things are now.

The card takes me over an hour to make, but I'm pleased with my efforts. I quickly get changed out of my pyjamas into leggings and a hoodie and head downstairs, where I meet Mum in the hall. She's heading into the front room with a mug of tea.

'Going out?' she says, surprised.

'Orla's birthday,' I say. 'I'm just dropping her a card.' I hold up my creation for her to see.

'Oh. That's very thoughtful of you, love.' She looks… sad, I think.

'I do it every year,' I say, acting like this isn't a last-minute effort to cover the fact I'd almost forgotten.

'Of course. Well, have a nice evening. Don't be late, sure you won't? It's to rain later.'

'I won't.'

A tingle of excitement rushes through me as I press Orla's doorbell and hear the familiar chime. I can't remember the last time I was here. I clutch the homemade card tightly in my hands, eager to see her reaction.

Angela answers the door. 'Freya!' she says. She's wearing a Rudolph apron with a big red nose on it. 'Orla said you weren't coming tonight. It's great to see you, love. They're all in the back room. Here, let me take your coat.'

They?

The hallway is an overpowering clash of offensive smells: greasy oven food, fake tan and boys' deodorant. I walk tentatively through the kitchen towards the back room, the sound of voices getting louder as I approach it. I hold my breath as I push open the door, not sure what to expect on the other side. My eyes widen as I take in the scene: a group of girls, mostly from school, and boys (who on earth are they?) sprawled across the sofa, chairs and floor, sipping fizzy drinks from plastic cups and picking from bowls of crisps and sweets. Above their heads, a banner reads, 'HAPPY BIRTHDAY, ORLA!!' In the middle of the scene is Orla, sitting at the edge of the coffee table, wearing an off-the-shoulder pink top and white jeans. She turns to see who has entered, and her giant grin slips and shatters as she realises it's me. Her expression is almost comical, and I might laugh if I wasn't frozen from shock. I hold her birthday card close to anchor me. Then Izzo spots me and makes her way over.

'Oh hi, *Freya*,' she says in that same saccharine voice she used when I last met her. She leans in to hug me and I tense as her smelly fake-tan arms drape loosely over my shoulders. 'It's so nice to see you. I'm so happy you made it.' She blinks at me. Her fake eyelashes look like bushy black caterpillars wriggling across her eyelids.

'I didn't know...'

'That tonight was Orla's party? Oh yeah, she's been planning it for weeks.'

She smiles sweetly at me, and I think she must be relishing my confusion.

Orla comes over to us. She looks like she's seen a ghost.

'Happy birthday,' I say mechanically, and thrust the card – the stupid, childish card – in her direction.

'Thanks,' she says awkwardly.

'Aw, Freya,' Izzo says, snatching the card from Orla's hand. 'Did you make this all by yourself? It's so *special*.'

The way she says the word 'special'... I know she's trying to hurt me with it. If she's still cross with me about Irish College, it would be easier if she just said so, because I don't understand whatever game she's playing instead.

'I have to go,' I say, locking a stupidly big grin to my face in a bid to appear unfazed by everything. 'Happy birthday!'

'Freya,' Orla says as I quickly make my way through the kitchen and back to the hall. I don't look back at her. I don't even acknowledge Angela when she says something about staying for cake. All I can think is, *I have to get out of here. I have to get home.*

I make it as far as the gate when I realise that it's raining and that my coat is still inside. I turn back and am just about to ring the doorbell when I hear voices in the hall. It's Orla and Angela. They're arguing.

'Why did you let her in?' Orla says.

'What did you expect me to do, close the door in her face? And why didn't you invite her in the first place? I thought we agreed that you were going to start making more of an effort with her, after all she's been through.'

'I invited her over for a movie tomorrow. Isn't that enough? You're the one who's suddenly obsessed with her. We're not even friends anymore.'

'That's enough, Orla,' Angela says sternly. 'Now go and give that poor girl back her coat before she catches her death.'

I quickly race back towards the gate so as not to startle Orla when she opens the door.

'Freya,' she calls. 'You forgot your coat.'

'Oh, thanks.'

She hands it to me without saying anything, and when I realise that she's about to close the door in my face, something comes over me and I speak.

'I don't care if you don't like me anymore!' I blurt. The words are frantic and urgent, practically tripping over themselves.

They take me by surprise completely. 'I never did anything bad to you, so I don't care if you don't like me anymore.'

Orla glances around, evidently unsure how to respond. 'Um, what?'

'I said I don't care if you don't like me anymore!'

'OK, well…'

'I don't care if you don't like me anymore!' I say again. The words are bursting to come out of me. I could say the same thing a hundred times over. 'I don't care if you–'

'Yeah, I heard you, Freya. I have to go.'

Orla closes the door and I'm left standing in the rain, my mouth twitching as I try to restrain my words for once. I could laugh or cry or scream right now, and it wouldn't matter which. These are my words. They might not be the most inspiring or powerful words ever spoken, but they're mine and for once they've found me on time.

Chapter 32

My fists pound the mattress so hard the springs sound and I quickly work up a sweat. I don't know how else to release the hot emotion bubbling inside me.

She had a secret birthday party.

POUND POUND POUND.

She didn't want me there.

POUND POUND POUND.

She only invited me over tomorrow because Angela made her.

POUND POUND POUND.

She said we weren't friends anymore.

POUND POUND POUND POUND POUND.

I keep pounding until my wrists get sore and I'm breathless. I'm still wearing my coat, my shoes. I curl onto my side, my face next to Elsa's on my *Frozen* duvet cover. I trace the outline of her large blue eyes with my fingers, her sharp cheekbones. I'd have frozen everything in sight tonight if I were her. What exploded from me just now was enough to freeze over the entire country.

I lie still as my breathing steadies, let the silence of my room settle over me like an invisible blanket. It takes me a moment to register the gentle knocking on the door.

'Freya?' It's Dad. He enters and sits gingerly at the end of my bed. 'Are... are you all right?'

I sit up beside him. 'Orla had a secret birthday party and didn't invite me. She said we're not friends anymore.'

'Oh,' Dad says. 'I'm sorry, Freya. That... Well, that wasn't very nice of her.'

'No, it wasn't,' I say, surprisingly calm now. The hot emotion has subsided.

'Are you upset? Should we talk about it?'

I shake my head. 'Even when I cut off all my edges and make myself as tiny as possible, I still don't fit in. Even when I make myself as identical to them as possible, it's still not enough. What's the point?'

Dad brings his hand to his face reflexively, like he's trying to think of an answer.

'It's like there's some secret code that they all know and I don't, some invisible rule book that only I can't see. I tried so hard to understand them, but they never tried to understand me back, even when they learned the word to help them.'

I think about Shannon reading about autism to understand me better. About Chloe and her cousin, Rossa and Emma. People either open the door to learning about people who are different to them, or they close it. Orla's door has been firmly closed for a long time, but for some reason I've continued knocking on it, hoping for a response.

'They treat me like there's something wrong with me, but they're the ones who are wrong. And do you know what the worst part is? I wouldn't have wanted to go to Orla's smelly party even she had invited me. She went to all that effort to keep me away from something I would have tried to escape from in five minutes anyway. I don't want the things that she wants. I don't want to be like her and her new friends, and I don't want to pretend I do anymore. It's too hard.'

I exhale loudly and bask in the relief of it. My head feels refreshingly clear.

Dad shifts awkwardly beside me. I can feel him trying to think of something to say. 'You've certainly had a lot on your...'

'Don't say the plate thing,' I warn him.

'Oh, right. Sorry.'

Poor Dad. He's really borne the brunt of chit-chat chores this week.

'I just think it's a silly expression,' I explain. 'Nobody is walking around with a plate in their hands, topping it up with problems. The world isn't a giant problem buffet.'

Dad laughs. 'It is a silly expression, isn't it?'

I smile. 'Yeah. And if your plate was too heavy, why wouldn't you just put it down? Why would you keep carrying it around everywhere? It makes no sense.'

Dad looks down at the pages of sketches littering my bedroom floor. 'You've been busy up here the last few days. Who are these little fellas?' He crouches down and picks up one of the sketches.

'The characters from *Inside Out.*'

'And this one?'

'That's a changeling,' I say, sliding my hands under my legs instinctively.

'A changeling. Very unusual.'

'We learned about them in Slievanure. P.J. Browne was talking about them. He said that changelings were probably just autistic children, or children with other disabilities, but people didn't understand that at the time. The only way they could explain their children's differences was by imagining they had been swapped out with evil fairies when they were babies.'

Dad sets the sketch down gently. 'That's sad,' he says quietly. 'At least things are better nowadays.'

'But they're still not good enough,' I say, feeling that same emotion rumble in my belly again. 'Autistic people are still being excluded and left behind.' I think about Rossa's family's struggle to find Emma a place in school because there are no autism classes in their area. 'People don't understand enough about autism, and because they don't understand, they don't care.'

Dad nods. 'You're right. To be honest, that's why I was

apprehensive when we first started talking about having you assessed.'

I think back to the conversations I'd eavesdropped on in the kitchen during the summer, Dad trying to reassure Mum that I was just a normal teenager going through normal teenager problems. Was he trying to convince himself?

'Why were you apprehensive?' I ask.

Dad exhales. 'It's a complicated word, autism. It's so bogged down with negativity and fear. I could see how it made sense for you – I knew all the things you were struggling with – but I was worried that people wouldn't understand what it really meant. I was worried that a diagnosis might only make things harder. I remember looking at different checklists with Mum, trying to see if we recognised any signs or traits in you, and feeling so disheartened by how negative they all were. All these so-called 'red flags' like *rigid interests* and *unusual play behaviours*. Who decided that those things were red flags anyway?' Dad shakes his head. 'I don't think it's fair on anyone – autistic people or their families – that a diagnosis is made to seem like the end of the world, when the real problem is the world not understanding and supporting autistic people, like you said.'

I think about the leaflets in Ms Connolly's office; the images of shadowy children and scattered puzzle pieces. There was never any hope in those pictures, only doom. Dad was right; any parent would feel scared about their child being autistic when that's how it was always depicted.

'I'm glad you're starting to feel better about things,' Dad offers. 'I know it's a lot to make sense of, but we only ever wanted a diagnosis to be helpful for you.'

'I know. I just... really didn't want to be different.'

'Different's not bad though. It's just different. Everybody is different. That's what makes the world an interesting place.'

Dad sounds like a children's TV presenter about to break into song.

'You're so cheesy,' I say, unable to hide my smile.

'Really? I thought that sounded good! I came up with it on the spot.'

'No way. You heard it somewhere before. In a nursery rhyme, maybe.'

'OK, how about this then: being different is so ordinary it's boring. You're a little bit different from some people, and other people are a little bit different from you. Big deal, who cares, get over it.'

'Wow. Definitely not cheesy. That's pretty good actually.'

'Thank you.'

'Do you think I should just get over it?'

Dad shrugs. 'I think you'd be happier if you could. It's a lot of work trying to match somebody else's definition of normal. Think of the fun you could have if you just embraced your own definition of the word.'

I've never thought about it in terms of fun.

'I know it takes courage,' he adds, 'to embrace a diagnosis so few people understand. But there's so much good that can come from this, if you can just find a way to see it.'

'That's what Mum always says.'

'I think she's right. I'm glad she didn't listen to me last summer. I was worried about other people, but she was only thinking about you. She was determined to help and understand as best as she could.'

I feel a small rise in my chest then, like my heart is looking around for something. I think I know what.

Chapter 33

Mum is flicking through a magazine at the kitchen table when I go to find her the next morning.

'Hi, love,' she says absently, half looking up at me. 'Had you a nice time at Orla's?'

I ignore the question and take a seat across from her.

'Are you all right?'

I nod. 'Well, actually…' The words I had planned to say are suddenly blurry in my mind. 'I… I'm sorry,' I say, clutching as many as I can before they disappear. 'For shouting and being cross. I'm sorry.'

Mum sets her magazine down. 'I'm sorry too. I feel like all I've been doing recently is giving out to you and making things worse.'

'But you were worried about me,' I say, surprised that Mum feels she has anything to apologise for.

'I was – *am* – that's true, but you're dealing with a lot and me being hard on you doesn't help things. I don't want to fight you, love. I want to be on your side.'

'But you're the most on my side of everyone,' I say, feeling flustered that she's misinterpreted things like this. 'You only ever try to help me. I'm sorry I said horrible things to you.'

Mum reaches her hand across the table and places it on mine. 'Thanks, pet. What are we like? Moping around like a pair of… well, you *are* a teenager. What's my excuse?'

The feeling of her hand on mine makes my heart calm. 'I'm sorry,' I say again.

Mum smiles. 'It's been a hard time for you, hasn't it, after everything in Irish College?'

Irish College. The words alone make my mind feel fizzy. 'Yeah.'

'I can see that. It's like everything came to a head, isn't it? It was probably building up in you since the summer.'

'How do people know what they're feeling?' I ask then. 'Do the words just pop up in their heads and then they know?'

Mum thinks for a moment. 'It's not always obvious, but usually when you think about it, or talk about it with someone, it becomes clear. Is that different to what you experience?'

Clarity and feelings are not things I would ever put together. For me, trying to name what I'm feeling is like rummaging my hand around in a hat of raffle tickets, eyes closed, and hoping I pick the right one.

'I don't really have words for feelings. I just feel them. Sometimes they're hot, or cold, or prickly, or soft. Sometimes I feel them all together and I can't separate them. Then they get clogged up inside me because I don't how to sort them. You know how Ms Connolly helps me with studying so that I'll be better at doing exams? I think I need help like that, but for feelings. I need to go to feelings school.'

Mum stifles a small laugh. 'Oh, love. I don't know about feelings school, but... what about therapy? It was probably too much last summer, but maybe you'd be better able for it now. What do you think?'

'You mean see Fiona again?'

'Or someone like her. Therapists can help you make sense of your emotions. They can help you identify them, understand them, deal with them.'

I think about this for a moment. 'You mean they can help me process them.'

Mum winks. 'Bingo.'

What Is the Spectrum?

Have you ever seen the colour cards for paint that show different shades of a particular colour from dark to light? Many people think that's what the autism spectrum is like; that it goes from dark (severe) to light (mild), and that, consequently, some people are 'more' or 'less' autistic than others. The reality is far more complex than that. I understand the desire to categorise differences among autistic people to make better sense of our community as a whole, but thinking of us as being on one side of a line or another, or in one box or another, is not a useful way to do this. Because I speak to communicate, I am viewed has being 'mildly' autistic and therefore less burdensome and more valuable to society than non-speaking autistics. Because I do not have any co-occurring conditions or disabilities, it is assumed that my autism is 'light' compared to others. It is true that I have comparably lower support needs to autistic people who are non-speaking, have motor planning difficulties or co-occurring disabilities, but that doesn't eliminate the sensory, social and emotional processing challenges that I've struggled with since I was a baby. Not always being able to see someone's differences does not mean they're not there. Similarly, not always recognising someone's potential beneath their challenges doesn't mean it isn't there. This is what thinking about autism as a linear spectrum of severe to mild does to autistic people: it only focuses on what's observable on the outside. As a result, some people's challenges are overlooked, while others' ability is written off completely. Everybody loses!

This is why I think we need to rethink the language around the autism spectrum and not rely on vague descriptors like 'mild' and 'severe' to fill in the blanks about people. There are no definitions for these terms anyway, and I don't believe they give the full picture of anyone. What does give the full picture is specific language to describe a person's strengths, challenges, and level of support needs. For example: My name is Rossa, my key strengths are my ability to focus intensely on subjects I care about and my strong sense of justice; my biggest challenges are sensory processing and social awareness, and I need support with task transitioning, organisational skills, and building friendships. That's more specific than 'mildly autistic', isn't it? If you knew me, wouldn't you have a better idea of how to support me now?

The language around autism matters. It should be centred around the person as they truly are, not what they appear to be on the surface. It should help others to understand us and provide direction for supporting us. Focusing on what autism means for the individual, rather than trying to rank all autistic people according to observable characteristics, is

a far more helpful way of building true understanding of our community.

Chapter 34

Shannon and I plan to meet at the library before school to set up our display before the official opening. She arrives after me, and I'm surprised by her appearance as she walks towards me in the corridor.

'Your hair,' I say, admiring the intricate braid running down her back. 'And your make-up!'

Shannon twirls proudly to show off her efforts. 'Not every day the press shows up at school. That Zoe Turner cuts a good tutorial, doesn't she? Do you think the make-up is subtle enough? It's supposed to look natural. I don't want to have to wipe it off.'

'It's really subtle,' I reassure her.

Shannon smiles. 'Phew! Ready to head in?'

'Just a second,' I say, taking something out of my school bag. 'This is for you.'

I hand Shannon a homemade card with a sketch of her on the front.

Shannon stares at me, open-mouthed. 'You made this for me?'

'For when you become a writer. Someone in the future is

209

going to want to add your picture to a poster.'

'Oh my God, I love it! Thank you so much, Freya.'

'There's a note on the back,' I say, feeling myself blush.

Shannon turns the card over. '*Dear Shannon. Thank you for being good company in the hovel. From Freya.* This is *so* nice, Freya! I'm honestly so chuffed!'

'Glad you like it.'

'Seriously, thank you. I love it so much, you have no idea. Come on, we better get started on our display.'

Shannon pushes open the door to the new library and the smell of sawdust and fresh paint immediately overwhelms my nostrils. We step inside and it takes my eyes a few seconds to adjust to the brightness of the room, which has floor-to-ceiling windows all along the back wall. The floor is covered in a deep blue carpet with a squiggle design that makes it look covered in worms, and in the centre of the room is a cluster of white desks, each lined with lime green chairs that look hard and uncomfortable. In one corner, there's a reading nook with a scratchy-looking green sofa and beanbags.

'*Whoa,*' Shannon says, taking in the bright, open space. 'It's more amazing than I imagined. I can't believe this is in our school! OK, you're *definitely* not allowed to eat your lunch in here. This place is sacred!'

I force a small laugh. I don't think that will be a problem somehow. It turns out I *hate* the new library.

'Girls!' Ms Horgan makes her way over to us. 'Well, what do you think?'

'It's incredible!' Shannon says. 'I can't believe it's finally open. Totally worth the wait.'

'Aw, I'm glad you think so,' Ms Horgan says, sharing in Shannon's delight. 'I think it'll be a fantastic asset to the school. And talk about kicking things off in style! The Minister cutting the ribbon, the *Irish Times* taking photos. The library will be the place to be after this! Go on anyway, I'll leave you to set up.'

Shannon and I assemble our display alongside a few girls from other years. Ours is by far the best one, and I'm proud of the effort we've put in.

'Writing Teresa Deevy's name in sign language was genius, Freya,' Shannon says, gluing my sketch to the display board. 'It's such a nice way to acknowledge her Deafness. It must have taken you ages to do all the little hands.'

It had, but the challenge was a welcome distraction at the time.

'This is going to look amazing when we're done. And it's nice to say we finally did something on the Library Committee, eh?' Shannon says. 'Hey, are you OK?'

I realise I'm being quieter than usual. 'I'm fine,' I say. 'Just...'

'Nervous?' Shannon says, supplying the answer for me. 'It'll be fun. Plus, we get to miss class to be here, and Ms Horgan even said there'll be tea and biscuits after. They're really going all out for the Minister!'

All members of the Library Committee are called down for the official opening after small break. There are twelve of us in total, two girls from every year.

'All looking neat and tidy, girls,' Ms Dwyer, the principal, says, inspecting our uniforms before letting us inside. 'Take your seats and wait quietly until we're ready to begin. We have a very important guest joining us today, as you know, so absolutely no messing.' She gives us all a stern look.

The front-row chairs have 'reserved' signs on them, so Shannon and I sit in the row behind. We whisper a bit and look around, examine some of the other displays from a distance as a few teachers make final touches before the Minister arrives. There's excitement in the air, and it mingles with the smells of paint and sawdust swirling inside my head.

A few minutes later, there is movement outside and the Minister walks through the door, a professional-looking minion following behind her. There is also a man wearing a camera with a gigantic lens around his neck. We instinctively quieten down as they take their seats, the atmosphere feeling suddenly very serious. My gaze is focused squarely on the Minister, who looks powerful in a sharply-cut trouser suit and blue heels. When she sits in the chair directly in front of me, I can't help holding my breath. Shannon nudges me and mouths, *oh my Gooooood!*

Ms Horgan steps forward with the Chairman of the Board of Management and tells the whole story of how the new library came to be; the parents who campaigned for it for years, the local businesses that donated to the fund. She talks about what an important day this is for the students, and how important libraries are in all schools.

'And of course, we are just *honoured* to be able to share today with Minister for Education, Helena Carmody, a person who works tirelessly on behalf of Ireland's schools and students, and who is, of course, a dear friend to Leslie Park.' Ms Horgan welcomes the Minister to the front of the room, and we all applaud on cue.

Minister Carmody faces the crowd confidently, her palms faced open as she begins to speak. 'Well, let me just say that it's my absolute *pleasure* to be here today to open this *gorgeous* library, although I must admit, I *am* a bit jealous. I'm a proud Leslie Park girl, but I can tell you there was nothing like this back in my day. You girls are extremely lucky.' She raises an eyebrow as she glances around at us students, then plasters a huge grin to her face and laughs jokingly. We all laugh eagerly with her. At the side of the room, the photographer snaps picture after picture.

After the Minister has finished speaking, Ms Horgan invites everyone to have tea. The students linger until the adults have served themselves, then we wander over to the refreshments table. I pour myself a glass of water, while Shannon loads a paper plate with biscuits. 'Want any?' she asks. I surprise myself by taking a pink wafer.

Ms Horgan instructs us to stand in front of our displays so that the Minister can come around and talk to us. I feel twitchy all of a sudden, watching the Minister as she flits from one display to the next, the photographer following closely behind and taking the names of every girl he photographs on a small notepad.

'How's my hair?' Shannon asks as they approach us.

I smile and nod. I want to tell her it looks perfect, but the words don't come.

'Oh, wow,' the Minister says as she steps in front of our display. 'Isn't this fantastic? I love the artwork.'

'Freya did that,' Shannon says enthusiastically. 'The whole thing was her idea. There's this poster upstairs of all male Irish writers and we wanted to showcase women writers.'

The Minister nods approvingly. 'Talk about girl power!' she says, making a triumphant fist. The camera flashes right at that moment and then the photographer is asking for our names. The Minister wanders off and I realise that that's it, the moment is over. I was too stunned to even notice.

Ms Connolly tells us to say our goodbyes and to head back to our classrooms. We begin filing out of the library, the Minister waving politely at us as we go. Then, the photographer calls out, 'I just have one more idea for a shot, if we can hang onto one of the girls for a minute.' I don't let the opportunity pass me by.

Chapter 35

'Over here,' the photographer instructs me, and leads me towards the floor-to-ceiling windows.

I still can't believe I volunteered myself for this job, that I actually raised my hand and cried, 'ME!'

'I want you to be showing something to the Minister, just grab any book from the shelf. I'm going to step outside and get the shot through the window, really show off the architecture of the new building.'

The Minister is smiling next to me, but I can feel an air of impatience about her.

I grab a book from the shelf and open it in front of us. It is, of all things, a book about fairies.

'That's it,' the photographer says as he makes his way through the exit door and out of the building. 'Big smiles!'

'So, what do *you* think of the new library?' the Minister asks, a large grin on her face and palms open again. 'Isn't it *fantastic*?'

'I prefer the old one,' I say without thinking, then quickly try to back track. 'I mean, this one is… incredible. I can't believe it's *finally* open. Totally worth the wait.' That was what Shannon had said to Ms Horgan, wasn't it?

'That's great. God, you'll be spoiled for choice with all the books in here!'

She is theatrical in her gestures and facial expressions as she looks around, aware, I suspect, of the photographer snapping pictures of us from outside.

I know I should muster up some meaningless line of small talk, but I can't. I volunteered for this opportunity to be alone with the Minister for Education for a reason. I have something far more important to talk to her about and only seconds to do it.

'You need to open more autism classes,' I tell her urgently. 'There aren't enough in the country and hundreds of autistic children aren't in school because of it. It's wrong and you need to fix it.'

The Minister looks momentarily taken aback, then slides expertly back into control. 'Looks like we have a little politician on our hands,' she says in a singsong voice, pretending to be impressed with me.

I ignore her. 'Autistic people have the same rights as everyone else, but there aren't enough classes in Ireland to support their different needs. It's not fair. You have to do something.'

The Minister glances around and communicates something to the snap-happy photographer with her eyes. He sets his camera down. She turns back to me then, crouches forward and fixes a sympathetic smile to her face. 'Have you someone in your family on the spectrum, pet?'

I shake my head. '*I'm* autistic.'

'Oh,' she says, looking surprised and… possibly a bit confused. 'Well, you must be able to cope in a normal class.'

'Mainstream class,' I correct her. 'And I was barely coping before I started getting support this year. There are other autistic people who wouldn't be able to cope in a mainstream class though, who need more support than me. It's not fair that they don't get to go to school. You're failing them.'

The Minister straightens. 'Do you know something? I am *so* glad that I met you today,' she says, ushering me away from our photoshoot spot. 'You're absolutely right, and I can promise you that my department is doing everything we can to support people living with autism so that they get the same opportunities as everyone else.' She smiles and claps me on the arm, tells me it was a pleasure to meet me, then drifts away towards her minion before I get a chance to respond.

Rossa's mum is right. Trying to get through to politicians is like trying to get through a brick wall.

Chapter 36

At lunch time, the new library is packed with students exploring it for the first time, excitedly chatting among themselves as they scour the bookshelves, try out the new furniture and check out the Library Committee exhibitions. Ms Horgan moves around the room talking to everyone, a huge grin on her face as she flits from group to group. I can see that today is a huge day for our school; the new library is something people have been talking about since way before we were even in First Year. I don't want to hate it, but I can't help wishing I were back in the hovel. Shannon, meanwhile, is almost as excited as Ms Horgan, and proudly shows off our exhibition to anyone who passes by.

'Over here!' she calls, spotting Joy, Fatimah and Eva.

'So, this is the famous poster!' Joy says, impressed. 'Looks amazing, guys!'

'Freya, your sketches are awesome!' Fatimah says. 'I love all the little details.'

'Are those bees?' Eva asks, leaning in to see my sketch of Soinbhe Lally closer.

'Oh, you *have* to read a book this woman wrote,' Shannon

says. 'It's called *A Hive for the Honeybee* and it's basically like *Animal Farm* but with bees. We found a copy of it in one of the boxes of old books and Freya liked the idea of drawing bees.' She smiles at me.

'This one is in Irish,' Fatimah remarks, pointing to the biography under Peig Sayers' portrait. 'Did you write this, Shannon? Nóirín would be so proud!'

'I may have enlisted the help of Joy,' Shannon admits.

'Hardly,' Joy says. 'You nailed it all by yourself.'

'So, who was your favourite one to draw, Freya?' Eva asks me.

I scan the display and try to choose one. The truth is, I like all of them and I feel proud of my efforts. The exhibition had come along at exactly the right time.

'I liked drawing Maeve Brennan,' I say. 'Just because she's so elegant. And I've never drawn someone looking over their shoulder before. It was a good challenge.'

'Maeve Brennan was this seriously glamorous Irish writer living in New York in the 1940s,' Shannon explains. 'She wrote for the *New Yorker* and *Harper's Bazaar* and hung out with fancy people at cocktail parties. Some people even say she was the inspiration for Audrey Hepburn's character in *Breakfast at Tiffany's*.'

'I love that movie!' Fatimah says. 'And I can see the resemblance. They both have that oversized ballerina bun.'

'Yeah, but Maeve has way more edge than Holly Golightly,' Shannon says.

'I've never seen *Breakfast at Tiffany's*,' Eva says.

'OK, we're going to correct that ASAP,' Fatimah says. 'Everyone needs to see *Breakfast at Tiffany's*.'

'I've never seen it either,' Joy says.

'Maybe we could all watch it together sometime,' Shannon suggests.

'Ooh, we could start a film club!' Eva says.

'Yes!' Fatimah exclaims. 'Something Clever is back together again! We could watch it after exams maybe.'

The reminder makes everyone groan.

'I better go over my science notes,' Joy says.

'Yeah, I should probably look over my verbs for French,' Eva says.

'Well done on the poster, gals,' Fatimah says.

'So, what was your photoshoot with the Minister like?' Shannon asks after they've left. 'Is she more intimidating one-to-one?'

'Not really,' I say. 'I think she just wanted to leave.'

'I bet her cheeks must've hurt from all the professional smiling by then.'

'Yeah.'

I don't know if Minister Carmody listened to a word I said, but I'm glad I said something. It's like Rossa says; if enough people try, then maybe change can happen. I'd like to be a part of that change.

No, I'm Not Like Rain Man

I've never been particularly good at maths. I've never struggled with it in school, but I've never excelled at it either. Some of my classmates seem to have a natural ability for it, but I've always been somewhere in the middle. Being autistic, my lack of love or special talent for maths is something people sometimes struggle to believe. For example, once, when I failed to complete a long division question on the white board in primary school, my teacher reprimanded me for being lazy and told me to 'try harder, Rain Man.' I had to ask my mam what he meant when I went home.

For those who don't know, *Rain Man* is a film from the 1980s about an autistic savant called Raymond Babbitt. Raymond has special abilities, like being highly skilled with numbers and having an extraordinary memory. The film is widely credited with putting autism 'on the map' in popular culture, and many people appreciate its role in creating awareness of autism in the media at a time when there was otherwise very little. I think it's great that the film had a positive impact for some people, but unfortunately, it also perpetuates the myth that autistic people are all gifted or geniuses, when we aren't. (Nor should we have to be, to be accepted in society!).

I doubt the makers of *Rain Man* ever intended for it to be The One and Only Depiction of Autism Ever, but that's kind of what it has become. It's what our society has allowed it to become because we lack the curiosity to examine our collective understanding of autism more closely. Not all autistic people are savants, and not all savants are autistic. (On that note, it's probably worth mentioning that the man *Rain Man* is based on, Kim Peek, is not even believed to have been autistic). Not all autistic people have special skills and talents. Not all autistic people are white or male. Since there is no one way to be autistic, it makes no sense that we rely so heavily on one reference to capture the autistic experience.

That's why I think we need to hear from autistic people from all walks of life, of all ages, genders, races and ethnicities. There's a saying in the autistic community that goes, 'if you meet one autistic person, that's it: you've met one autistic person.' Isn't that an exciting thought? Why limit yourself to one representation of autism when there are so many other voices out there, waiting to be heard, if only people would listen?

Chapter 37

Tom's arrival home for Christmas is as hurricane-like as we might have predicted. He landed in Dublin the weekend before my exams and had to beg for a last-minute lift when he realised he had no money for the bus, derailing Mum and Dad's Christmas shopping plans and creating a flurry of stress in the house. When he finally does make it home, however, his charmingly chaotic energy brightens the house like fairy lights and all is forgiven.

'Where's the tinsel?' he asks, plonking his suitcase on the living-room floor and eyeing the Christmas tree disapprovingly.

Mum fidgets with the pendant on her necklace. 'Well, Freya and I were watching a programme on the telly the other night, and the interior designer said tinsel was out this year.'

Tom shakes his head. 'I'm not even *entertaining* this. Where is it?' He marches out of the room.

'You weren't even here for decorating,' I argue, watching as Tom rummages through the decoration boxes at the foot of the stairs.

'Doesn't matter. Christmas is not about being trendy. It's about keeping things the exact same every year.'

'Well, it's about more than that,' Dad interjects. He watches, amused, as Tom marches back to the tree with the tinsel and begins clumsily draping it over the branches.

'It looks like giant, glittery worms are eating the tree,' I say.

'That,' Tom huffs, 'is the whole point.'

I don't tell him that that makes no sense. In fact, I don't actually mind that Tom is undoing my and Mum's work at all. Tom's right: the age-old, thinning ropes of tinsel are a staple of Christmas in our house. That's what makes them lovely, even though they look more like wire cleaners these days.

Satisfied with his tinsel efforts, Tom turns his attention to the rest of the tree and begins rearranging the decorations to his liking. 'Remember this?' he says, plucking a clear bauble with a picture of us visiting Santa from one of the branches. 'Remember the Lightning McQueen toy you got that made you cry?'

Cars was one of few Disney films I took a while to warm to. 'I didn't cry,' I correct him. 'I just told him I didn't want it.'

Tom laughs. 'Oh, yeah. I forgot your habit of rejecting gifts you don't like.'

Obviously, I understand now that it's rude to hand back gifts you don't like, but it seemed reasonable when I was a child. And I doubt Santa was offended. I recall him discreetly passing the toy to Mum to hide in her handbag.

'Don't mind him,' Mum says. 'I love that photo of you. The

little red cheeks on you both.'

'Remember when she used to order people out of the house too?' Tom continues. 'I remember Dad's cousin, Mary Rose, coming to stay and Freya repacking her suitcase for her and telling her to get out, like some evil landlord from the 1800s.'

Mum stifles a laugh. 'Poor Mary Rose hadn't even been with us a day.'

'You'd kick her out too if it was your room she was staying in,' I say, pretending to be offended even though I'm secretly enjoying the attention.

'Of course we would, Freya,' Mum says sensitively, and I realise I actually do sound offended.

'So, when are we opening the first presents?' Tom asks.

'Christmas Eve,' I say. 'Same as always.'

'Ah, but that's still a bit away. Why don't we just do one present now?'

'I thought Christmas was about things being the same every year,' Dad remarks from the sofa.

'Yes, but this Christmas is different,' Tom says. 'It's the first time I've come home for it. I think that calls for a new tradition. Or at least a little wiggle room on some of the old ones.'

The rest of us look at each other, as if taking a silent vote.

'Fine by me,' Dad says. 'Will we do one each?'

Mum kneels down by the tree and rummages among the carefully wrapped gifts. 'Right. Who's going first?'

'Why don't we give Dad whatever random book on local history he's bought for himself but is pretending is from you and get it out of the way,' Tom says.

Dad snorts with laughter.

'I have *no* idea what you're talking about,' Mum says, swatting Tom's leg playfully.

We watch as Dad unwraps a thin blue paperback. '*The Corcorans of Rathfarnam!*' he says, feigning surprise. '*How* did you know?'

It's hard not to laugh at his reaction. Dad isn't a naturally funny person, which makes his attempts at humour all the more entertaining to the rest of us.

'How indeed,' Tom says.

'Right, smart mouth,' Mum says, turning her attention to Tom. 'Would you like to go next?'

Tom closes his eyes and holds out his hands like a child. Mum places a neat box in them. 'Wow,' he says dryly, unwrapping a Nivea Men wash set. 'Thanks for the annual hint.'

'It's to take back with you,' Mum explains, as if she hasn't bought this gift on autopilot every year since Tom hit puberty. 'See? It even comes with a little travel bag.'

'Amazing. You've truly outdone yourself.'

Mum wrinkles her nose at him.

Theirs is a type of humour I could never pull off. Tom sounded playful and funny when he was being sarcastic, and Mum bounced off it. I sounded sulky and rude, and it put her on edge.

'Now then, Freya. Would you like a little present?'

'Hold on,' Dad says, making his way to the tree. 'Something for the lady of the house first.'

Tom and I look at each other. This was unusual.

Dad reaches to the back of the tree and retrieves a small gold box. Even Mum is surprised.

'For me?' she says, and begins untying the velvet ribbon. 'I hope it's not a Joni Mitchell CD.' She winks at me. We watched *Love, Actually* this week. (I took several toilet breaks to avoid the sex scenes).

Mum lifts the lid of the box and holds up a necklace, a light green stone on a gold chain.

'I saw it in the Powerscourt Centre one day,' Dad explains. 'I thought it was nice.'

'It's beautiful,' Mum says, fixing it around her neck. 'You didn't have to.'

'Consider it a gift from all of us. A thank you for all that you do.'

The tenderness in Dad's voice, the thoughtfulness of the gesture. I find it quite moving.

Mum smiles. 'God help the poor woman who got the Joni Mitchell CD,' she jokes, reaching over and squeezing Dad's hand. *Thank you,* she mouths.

'Freya's turn,' Tom says, setting things back on track.

Mum passes me something soft in snowman wrapping paper. 'It's only something small,' she says. 'A little goodluck charm for your exams.'

'Big perk of being in college,' Tom says smugly. 'No exams until after Christmas.'

'Does that mean you'll be studying while you're home?' Dad asks.

'What's that new book about again, Dad?' Tom asks, changing the subject.

'Ahem,' Mum says. 'Can we get back to Freya please?'

I pick the Sellotape off my present and am surprised to find a plush Belle doll on a keychain inside.

'I know it's not the same as your other one, but I thought... well, it's the same character, isn't it?'

My porcelain Belle doll. She must have spotted it broken in my room. I couldn't bring myself to throw it out.

'Thank you,' I say, taking in the details of my present. This is a very odd-looking Belle, with a disproportionately large head and huge bug eyes; she couldn't be less like my porcelain Belle. She's completely wrong in so many ways, but somehow, she's just right too. 'I love it.'

Mum smiles. 'It's only small. I saw it in one of the shops and thought of you.'

What Mum doesn't realise is that this is what makes wrong-Belle perfect. 'Thank you,' I say again.

Chapter 38

Exam week passes in a blur of late-night memorising and early-morning cramming, all of which proves worth it in the end as I manage, for the first time since starting secondary school, to get everything on paper in time. I'm even confident that I interpreted most questions correctly. Ms Connolly said I could bring the visual timer into the hall with me if I wanted, but I ended up creating my own for each exam and sketching them on the back of each paper instead for reference. They looked like multicoloured pizzas, with different colour highlighters indicating how much time I could spend on a particular section. I found it satisfying moving from colour to colour and checking with the clock on the wall that I was still on track. When Friday comes and we finish our last exams – Religion, Art and History for me – for the first time I don't feel full of dread. I didn't know the answer for everything, but at least I had a chance to answer what I did know.

The corridors are thrumming with excitement as everyone except the Fourth Years finish up exams after lunch. The music teachers have organised carols for the whole school to sing outside and I stand with Shannon, Joy, Fatimah and Eva as

Ms Breathnach and Mr Martinez hand out percussion instruments and sheet music. On the far side of the crowd, I spot Chloe, Orla and Izzo. Chloe spots me back and waves, but Izzo and Orla are busy checking their phones. More girls join the crowd and block them from view, which is probably for the best.

We get started with a couple of classics – 'Rudolph the Red-Nosed Reindeer', 'Jingle Bells,' 'Santa Claus Is Coming to Town' – and everyone is fired up for the finale of 'All I Want For Christmas Is You', which is loud and energetic and makes everyone laugh. Mr Martinez blushes furiously when the Sixth Years point to him and sing the chorus.

'Are we still going for hot chocolate?' Shannon says to the group as the crowd begins to disperse. We had made a plan on the morning of our first exams to celebrate at the end by going to Butler's.

'Pleeeease,' Joy says. 'I'm going to freeze if we don't go soon.'

They start making their way and I tell them that I'll catch up in a bit, I have something to do first.

'Come in,' Ms Connolly says when I knock on her door. 'Freya. Good to see you. How did you get on this week?'

'Good,' I say, taking a seat. 'I finished everything in time. I drew my own clocks and they worked; I finished every paper.'

'That's fantastic! Well done you. All the hard work paid off. I meant to say, fabulous photo in the paper of you and Minister Carmody. She looks so engrossed in whatever you're saying to her. And the library looks great, doesn't it? The photographer really captured the new building well.'

'I wanted to ask you about that,' I say, little butterfly wings starting to beat in my chest.

'Oh?'

'Well, it's just that the new library is… bright. And busy. And echoey.'

'I see,' Ms Connolly says.

'I know it's really good that we have it and we're really lucky and everything, but…'

'You prefer the old one?'

I nod. 'I was thinking, maybe, if it's still empty, we could keep it as a quiet space for people who need it. People… like me. It could be a place to go to if you feel overwhelmed in school.'

'That's a lovely idea,' Ms Connolly says. 'I think we'll still need to use it for storage, but I'm sure we could reserve a section for students. I can already think of a few who might benefit from it. Leave it with me and I'll look into it.'

'Thank you,' I say. 'And thank you for all your help this year. School is…' I tug at my sleeve '…getting better.'

Ms Connolly smiles. 'I'm glad to hear that, Freya. I really am.'

Shannon and the others are sitting on sofas near the back of Butler's when I arrive. They already have their hot chocolates and I go to the counter to order mine. A voice in my head tells me I shouldn't, but I swat it away. It would be worse to be the only one without a hot chocolate.

'You're just in time,' Shannon tells me. 'We've just finished the exam post-mortems.'

I take a seat next to her and notice the speaker playing music above us. We're also sandwiched between the coffee counter, which is noisy from all the different machines, and the bathrooms, which have a steady stream of people coming in and out of them. It isn't ideal, but at least it's not the people I'm with that's putting me on edge.

'Would you say Butler's is the best hot chocolate going?' Eva says. 'I would say that it's the best hot chocolate going.'

'Hard disagree,' Joy replies.

'Here we go,' Fatimah says.

'It scores high for flavour and consistency, but the marshmallow situation…' Joy shakes her head. 'Two full-size marshmallows that don't melt and you have to pay extra for? No. It loses points for that.'

'Fair point,' Shannon says. 'What would you say is the best then?'

'Insomnia, hands down. It's made with melted chocolate, not just generic powder, and they put loads of marshmallows and chocolate flakes on top. It's seriously underrated.'

'Yeah, but here you get a free truffle with your order,' Eva says. 'That cancels out the extra marshmallow cost in my opinion.'

'That's an external factor,' Joy argues. 'It doesn't improve the hot chocolate itself.'

'But it enhances the overall hot chocolate *experience*,' Fatimah says.

'Yeah,' Eva agrees, 'and that's what Butler's is all about. They're specialised chocolatiers, not a coffee chain that sells sad fridge paninis.'

They all groan at 'sad fridge paninis.'

'You're falling for the marketing,' Joy says. 'I bet if we did a blind taste test, Insomnia would win. I'm telling you, it's a gem hiding in plain sight.'

In my brain, a little person is sorting every comment like it's a package at a post office. I have no idea what to do with all of this information, but I'm hoping a perfect window of opportunity to include myself will open soon.

'Criteria for an excellent hot chocolate,' Shannon says, and they all think seriously.

'Hot,' Eva says, causing Joy and Fatimah to splutter with laughter.

'Well, yeah,' Joy says. 'I can't imagine anyone's ideal hot chocolate is cold.'

'Do you also favour a brown coloured hot chocolate?' Fatimah says. 'Or are you more partial to a shade of blue?'

'Mmm, cold blue chocolate,' Joy says.

'OK, you're both *this* close to getting flicked in the temple,' Eva says.

'There's such a thing as frozen blue hot chocolate,' I say, and they all turn to look at me.

Keep going, I will myself. *Put another penny in the slot.*

'Well, it's not frozen as in cold; it's *Frozen*, as in, the Disney movie. It's made with white chocolate and blue food colouring. I saw a picture of it on Instagram once.'

'I need to see this,' Shannon says, taking out her phone and typing something onto her screen. 'Oh my God,' she says, turning her screen around to show us.

'Ewww,' Joy says, peering in closer. 'It looks like paint water with glittery whipped cream on top.'

'It looks like Head and Shoulders shampoo that's been lathered up,' Eva says. 'And yeah, covered in glitter for some reason.'

'Is it weird that I think it looks kind of delicious?' Fatimah says.

'Have you ever had this, Freya?' Shannon asks.

I shake my head. I couldn't look at the picture for too long when I came across it last year. It made me feel queasy. The thought of me drinking such a thing is preposterous, but Shannon doesn't know about my food problem.

'I guess we'll have to expand the criteria for an excellent hot chocolate,' Joy says. 'It turns out colour may vary.'

'Sorry, Eva,' Fatimah says, and blows her a kiss.

'Uh huh,' Eva says. 'At least Freya has my back.' She smiles at me.

I take a sip of my hot chocolate, which is sweet and delicious, and try to savour the taste along with this very pleasant moment.

Chapter 39

I'm putting the last touches to the handmade calendars I've made for my family for Christmas when Mum appears at my door. 'Can I come in?' She sounds unusually formal. She takes a seat on the chair beside my desk. 'So, I was on to Fiona this week about you going to meet her again. She said she'd be able to see you in the new year, if you'd be on for it. She suggested a weekly meeting for a few weeks to see how you get on together. What do you think?'

'She thinks she can teach me how to figure out my emotions?'

Mum nods. 'She hopes she'll be able to help. She said she has different resources and ideas she'd like to explore.'

'OK.' The idea is surprisingly pleasant.

'Wonderful,' Mum says. 'I'll call her back and let her know. There was something else I wanted to ask you.' Mum takes out her phone.

'I can't believe your background photo is me and the Minister,' I say, catching sight of her screen.

Mum pulls her phone towards her defensively. 'If I want my brilliant daughter taking on politicians to be my background photo, then I'll have it.' She smiles. 'Anyway, I wanted to show you an email I got earlier in the week. It's from an outpatient service for young people… with eating disorders.'

The room feels suddenly smaller when she says the words.

'You mightn't remember,' Mum continues, 'but after we left the hospital, the doctor went over a few treatment options with us. We put your name on a waiting list for this place and they've finally gotten in touch about a meeting.'

I feel prickly. This meeting doesn't sound nice like meeting Fiona sounds nice. 'But I'm better now,' I say. 'I had hot chocolate today. I haven't had that in ages. And I've been following the food plan again.'

'I know, pet,' Mum says, trying to sound encouraging, but falling short. 'But eating disorders are very serious things that can take a long time to recover from properly.'

'But I am recovering. It's just that after Irish College I didn't feel hungry because I was tired and sick, and my head was distracted.'

Mum looks pained, like she doesn't want to put up a fight. 'I know you think that, Freya, but remember, this is also what eating disorders do to a person. They're a bugger of an illness that have a way of controlling people's minds when they're vulnerable. They tell you to avoid food, to restrict, to lie. You've come so far in the last few months, love, but I think you need more support if you're to really beat this.'

As she's speaking, I start thinking about the difference between me last summer and me now. Only a few months had passed, but so much had changed. I was starting to feel like I belonged in the world, like there was a place for me here after all and I didn't have to twist myself out of shape to fit into it. But I'm also aware of the hand that's been hovering at the back of my mind all that time, a scary, skeletal thing that reaches for my thoughts when I feel out of sorts and tries to control them. It's been there for over a year now, and even though I've managed to avoid its grip these last few months, it's come close to catching me again. I can't be sure that it won't crack its knuckles and try again one day when I'm not expecting it.

'We can go to the meeting,' I say. 'I should go.'

Mum's face practically crumbles in relief. 'Oh, that's great. I'll email them back tomorrow. I know this is a lot, Freya, but I think this is the support you've needed. I think it's worth exploring our options to see what might be helpful. We'll take it all gently, I promise.'

I don't love the sound of attending an outpatient service at all, but I know that Mum is on my side. I know that she'd reach inside my head and break the fingers of that horrible hand if she could, but she can't. I need to do this for her – and Dad and Tom – as much as myself.

Four Things I'd Like People to Understand About Autism

1. Eye contact is hard

Eye contact is not a natural or comfortable communication style for many autistic people. For some, it is physically painful. For others, like me, it's distracting. I find it challenging enough to follow what another person is saying in conversation without forcing myself to look them in the eye too. Even though it might not appear that way, I am more likely to be listening to you if I'm not looking at you. I can pay better attention this way. Performative communication is not helpful for anyone, so why don't we all try to embrace autistic communication styles more instead?

2. Autistic people have empathy... sometimes too much

In my experience, autistic people feel things deeply, but we don't always express our feelings in a way that's typical of non-autistic people. For example, my love for nature is rooted in an empathy for the world around me so deep it often hurts. That's why I am an advocate for bees and other wildlife: I have to channel the pain I feel about climate injustice into something hopeful and pro-active. If I had less empathy, I would feel less passionately about the natural world than I do. Take it that my in-depth knowledge of several thousand species of bees = more empathy than I often know how to handle.

3. We are more than the stereotypes make us out to be

So many representations of autistic people in popular culture depict quirky maths geniuses who are inconvenienced by the existence of other people in the world. These exaggerated characters often state their age in days rather than years and are robotic in their mannerism. I feel very dismayed when I encounter this kind of autistic representation in books and TV because it doesn't reflect the authentic autistic experience as I know it. These caricatures created to be laughed at overlook the thoughtfulness, sensitivity, curiosity, creativity, imagination, humour and empathy of real autistic people. They reinforce the idea that we'd rather be alone, when so many of us desperately want friends and relationships. Autistic representation should help non-autistic people relate better to us, but sadly it often alienates us more from the rest of the population.

4. We move in our own ways

Autistic people move their bodies a lot. This is called stimming. It helps us to feel calm and in control of ourselves. Personally, I tend to skip when I'm walking and shake out my hands when I'm excited. I like the release stimming gives me. It helps me to process big emotions and feel balanced inside myself. People stare at me when I stim and sometimes I feel self-conscious. I'll try to do more subtle stims like pinching my skin or screwing my eyes tightly shut. I don't want to have to hide or suppress my stimming though. If people understood the autistic need to stim better, then maybe more of us could feel more confident to be our true selves.

Chapter 40

I wake early on Christmas morning and feel a surge of jitteriness as I remember what day it is. I picture Tom and me in the front room two hours from now (eight o'clock is our agreed time), poring over our gifts as morning light spills in gradually through the branches of the Christmas tree in the window. I picture Mum and Dad, puffy-eyed and yawning, clumsily tying the belts of their dressing gowns and trying to match our excitement in their sleepy faces. I picture the customary tray of tea and mountain of toast that Mum will carry in on the special Christmas tray and set down on the coffee table between us. Despite it rarely being as perfect a moment as I imagine – usually Tom and I squabble over something, or I get annoyed with Mum and her camera – memories of Christmas morning are ones I hold dear. Well, with the exception of last Christmas maybe.

Last Christmas, I was a couple of weeks into my food problems and figured the only way to get away with not eating mounds of meat, potatoes and gravy at dinner was to pretend that I was sick. I thought it would be a straightforward enough lie, but it involved us rescheduling the whole day for fear my pretend illness might be contagious. Our cousins, who usually visited our house on Christmas morning, wound up hosting Dad and Tom, while Mum stayed with me at home. It was additional stress that nobody needed, least of all Mum, who already had a whole day of cooking ahead of her. I remember watching from my bedroom window as she handed a shopping bag to Dad with the boxes of vol-au-vents and cocktail sausages she had bought for hosting. There was no point in us keeping them, and it meant my aunt and uncle didn't have to worry about feeding last-minute guests.

Mum felt bad for me, knowing how much I loved Christmas, and tried to make the day as cheerful as possible. She said we could watch a movie together while Dad and Tom were out, that she could time it for when everything was in the oven. I told her not to worry about me, that all I needed was sleep. At least that part was true; sleep was the only good thing I could give my body then, when I had begun depriving it of so much else.

Tom was visibly annoyed when he and Dad arrived home later that afternoon. Mum and I were in the kitchen, where I was watching her make stuffing.

'Well,' Mum said cheerily when they came in. 'Had you a nice time?'

'Lovely, yeah,' Dad said, removing his coat and hat.

'Grand,' Tom muttered. There was a lull of silence before

he spoke again. 'They were supposed to come here,' he said bitterly.

'Ah, I know, love,' Mum said. 'But we couldn't take the risk with Freya. She might be contagious.'

'She seems fine to me.'

Mum looked surprised. 'She was sick all day yesterday and could hardly eat a thing.'

'Nothing new there.'

'Tom,' Mum said sharply. 'That's not very nice.'

'Whatever. Call me when it's time for dinner.'

After Christmas dinner, the meal that had caused me so much turmoil, the mood began to lift. I joined my family for dessert, sipping quietly on peppermint tea and laughing along as they told terrible Christmas cracker jokes. Tom loosened up and Mum, in turn, relaxed a bit. Dad took out his old guitar and we attempted a few Christmas songs, him and Tom leading the way as Mum and I followed along timidly.

'Sing *Silent Night*, Freya,' Mum said then, her cheeks flushed from red wine. 'Your voice is so lovely. Please.'

After what I had put everyone through that day, I could hardly refuse.

Dad gave me an intro and accompanied me as I sang two verses shakily. In the corner of my eye, Mum quietly wiped tears away with her thumb.

'They're here,' Tom calls from the front room, where the two of us have been watching *Elf* while Mum and Dad prepare for our guests.

Mum hurries into the room, a trail of freshly-spritzed perfume in her wake. My nose wrinkles as it catches in my nostrils.

'For God's sake, put all that rubbish away, will you?' she says, indicating the *Miniature Heroes* wrappers piled high on the coffee table in front of Tom.

Tom dutifully slides the wrappers back in the tub and pushes it under the Christmas tree. 'All done. Looking lovely, mother dear.'

Mum ignores him. 'Freya,' she says, smoothing down her blouse self-consciously. 'Am I all right? Will I get away with this outfit?'

'You look lovely, Mum.'

The doorbell rings and soon the front room is full of energy as my aunt, uncle and cousins settle in and everyone gets chatting. Tom is the centre of attention, and everyone listens attentively as he talks about Manchester and being a student away from home. I am always amazed at how effortlessly he carries himself in conversation, how he can make silly jokes without ever sounding rude and manages to keep everyone's mood up. After a while, I sneak upstairs for some quiet.

I lie down on my bed and scroll through my phone. I like a picture Chloe posted of her new rollerblades and another one

Rossa posted of the stack of nature books he received. I sent Rossa a message yesterday, but I haven't heard back yet. In our group chat, Something Clever, more photos of presents have been sent in, and I add a photo of my new Disney Vans.

Joy: **Ahhh so cute!!**

Shannon: **Very Freya <3**

Eva: **A-dor-a-ble**

Fatimah: **Love these!! Also loving your Disney Christmas short film recs.** *The Little Match Girl* **is so sad though :(**

Joy: **Right?? But the music is so beautiful. I added it to my study playlist**

Shannon: **I loved** *Mickey's Christmas Carol.* **And those crazy 1930s films were so funny. I'm still trying to wrap my head around the fact that Mickey and Minnie – two mice – end up adopting a bunch of orphan kittens in one of them…??**

Eva: **Shhh you're overthinking it. PS Shannon that Dolly Parton Christmas film you recommended is the most delightfully cheesy thing in existence.**

Shannon: **Dolly truly is an Unlikely Angel. If I had a choice between her or Clarence from** *It's A Wonderful Life* **descending from heaven as my Christmas guardian angel, I'd choose Dolly every time.**

Eva: **Agreed. In Dolly we trust.**

Shannon: **Amen.**

Downstairs, Mum calls me to say goodbye to our cousins.

'That was lovely, wasn't it?' she says, gathering up the discarded festive napkins and stray cocktail sticks after they've left. She makes a pile on the coffee table, then stretches the small of her back before sitting down to take her heels off.

'Come on, let's put our feet up for a minute,' she says, patting the seat next to her on the sofa. 'And pass me one of those sausages, will you?'

I take a seat and reach for the serving plate. Mum leans forward and spears three honey-glazed sausages with a cocktail stick.

'Now this, for me, is what Christmas is all about,' she says, sinking into the back of the sofa and propping her feet on the coffee table. 'Just taking a minute, in the middle of the day, with a plate of leftover cocktail sausages.'

She passes the plate and I pick up a sausage. It is sticky with honey and cold to touch. I take it in small bites and am surprised by how much I enjoy it. I reach for another after that and pop it cleanly into my mouth without thinking.

Mum nods approvingly. 'Good?'

I smile between chews and sink back into the sofa beside her. 'Good.'

My phone vibrates in my pocket then and I take it out to find a message from Rossa.

Hello Freya, it's really nice to meet you. Thank you for your message. I'm glad you find my blog helpful. That's exactly

why I started it. That's really cool that your school is letting you design a sensory room for autistic students. I'm going to ask my followers what they think are the most essential things for a school sensory room and then I'll post a blog about it. Congratulations on your diagnosis, by the way. I hope it's been helpful for you. Welcome to the community!

'What has you all smiley?' Mum asks beside me.

'Nothing,' I say. 'Just messaging a friend.'

Chapter 41

Conversation around the dinner table is light-hearted and fun, fuelled mainly by Tom and Mum while Dad and I listen contentedly. Mum wants to know everything about Tom's housekeeping efforts in Manchester, and then regrets bringing it up when he fills her in.

'I'm just saying that if you soak the pots and pans as soon as you're done with them, you'll have an easier time scrubbing them clean afterwards,' she tells him.

'But then I'd have to transfer my dinner to a plate,' Tom says incoherently through a mouthful of potato.

'But sure, what else would you be doing with it?'

Tom swallows. 'Eating it directly from the pot, obviously. Why would I create more washing up for myself?'

Mum looks at Dad and me, appalled. 'What kind of animal have I reared at all?'

'One who's too frugal to waste precious washing up liquid,' Tom says, wiping bits of dinner from his stubble with the back of his hand.

'How's the turkey, Freya?' Mum asks, changing the subject. 'Not too dry, I hope.'

'It's tasty,' I say, slicing off another corner with my fork and dipping it in some cranberry sauce.

'A bit dry,' Tom teases, and Mum swats him with her napkin.

'Christmas cracker, anyone?' Dad says.

'Go on,' Tom says, and reaches out his hand. They pull on three and fall back into their chairs as it snaps.

'Yes!' Tom exclaims, waving the bigger part of the cracker in his hand. He unwraps the paper crown tucked inside and fishes out the prize of a disappointing-looking wire puzzle.

'What's the joke?' I ask.

Tom clears his throat dramatically as he holds up the small slip of paper. 'Yikes, this is bad even for a Christmas cracker. Why do birds fly south for the winter?'

'Because it's cold in the north,' I say, even though that's a fact, not a joke.

Tom sighs and announces the answer through gritted teeth. '*Because it's too far to walk.*'

Mum snorts. 'Ah, God. They've really gone to the dogs this year, haven't they?'

'But they wouldn't be able to walk,' I say.

Tom crumples up the paper and flicks it at my head. 'Duh, Freya. It's a *joke.*'

'But it's not a joke,' I say. 'It doesn't make sense.'

'It's from a *Christmas cracker*,' Tom says, as though I've missed something.

'It's still supposed to make sense.'

'Well, then you write to the good people of Christmas Cracker and Co. and tell them that.'

'You just watch her,' Mum says, proudly gesturing to the photo of me and Minister Carmody on the fridge. It's not enough that she has it on her phone; I have to face my face in the kitchen every day now too. 'Freya could run this country, if you ask me.'

'I really couldn't,' I say.

'Standing up to a minister is pretty badass, to be fair,' Tom says.

'She didn't even listen to me.'

'You don't know that,' Dad says. 'And it sparked the idea for the sensory room.'

'I didn't hear this part of the story,' Tom says.

'They're opening a sensory room in Leslie Park,' Dad says. 'Freya's idea. A way to support neurodivergent students in the school. Isn't that right?'

I nod sheepishly and slice into a Brussels sprout.

'Very cool,' Tom says. 'You'll have to keep me posted on it.'

I don't know when Tom found out that I'm autistic. I suspect Mum told him. I thought he'd roll his eyes when he found out – maybe he did – but he's been so generous and kind since he got home for Christmas. I can't remember when we last got on so well. This Christmas feels a million times lovelier than last year.

Chapter 42

The rest of the holidays pass in a pleasant haze of Disney movie marathons, games and walks with my family, drawing and messaging friends. Rossa and I message back and forth more frequently, and he collects some great ideas for the new sensory room. He tells me that his blog post on it is one of his most popular ones to date, with teachers all around the world sharing it. I print it off to show Ms Connolly on the first day back, although I imagine she's probably already read it online.

Returning to school after Christmas is never easy, but this year feels harder than usual when the break at home with my family was so nice. Our first official Something Clever film club meeting on Friday gets me through those first few days of classes, teachers, and noisy corridors.

'Freya,' Eva says, waving me over to the reading area in the new library.

They're all on the bean bags and I instinctively take a seat on the green sofa instead, slightly at a distance. I'm pleasantly surprised to discover that it's not as uncomfortable or scratchy as it looks.

We get talking about our January film, *When Harry Met Sally*, which Shannon suggested because it has 'big New Year's energy'.

'I'm *obsessed* with Sally's New York look,' Shannon says. 'The red turtleneck, the slacks, the brogues, the glasses. I'm here for all of it. That's going to be my whole aesthetic when I'm a novelist in New York. Or a playwright. I'm not sure which yet. Maybe both.'

'A playwright in New York?' Fatimah says. 'Um, will you write me a part in something so I can come too?'

'Of course! We can rent an apartment together. It'll be a leaky dump that probably has rats, but also kind of charming.'

'I want to go too,' Joy says. 'I could be a reporter for *The New York Times*.'

'And I'll… eat hot dogs from those carts on the side of the street and wander around looking at stuff,' Eva says. 'But in an artistic way.'

'Very Maeve Brennan,' Shannon says approvingly. 'Minus the hot dogs, I'm guessing. Freya, will you come too?'

'Sure,' I say. I have no idea what I would do in New York, but at least I'd have friends there.

We talk some more about the movie – about *Auld Lang Syne* and elderly couples and diners – and laugh about our imagined life in New York together. When a couple of serious-looking Sixth Years come in to study, we start to pack up.

'Should we head back to the common area until the bell rings?' Joy says.

Eva sighs. 'Yeah, I have to finish my English homework.'

We put our chairs away and head out.

'I'm just going to go upstairs for a bit,' I say to Shannon in the corridor.

'Oh, cool,' she says. 'See you at lunch? Maybe we can go for a walk outside again if the common area's too noisy.'

'Sounds good.'

'Awesome.' Shannon high-fives me and goes to catch up with the others.

The window in the door of the old classroom is covered with sugar paper now to make it more private. Inside, the old furniture has all been stacked to the side, leaving just enough room for a small sensory area. There isn't much by way of equipment yet, but Ms Connolly and a few of the other teachers sourced a rug, some floor cushions, a yoga ball, and a lamp that gives the room a soft, cosy glow. It's a pretty good start, and I can't think of anything else I'd even want. The most important thing is the space itself.

When I shut the door behind me, I see that Olivia, the autistic girl in First Year, is here already. She likes to read in here mostly, and I tend to sit on the other side of the blackboard divider we created so that we have space from each other. I haven't seen many other girls use this space yet, although a Fourth Year appears from time to time. I guess anyone who might need the sensory room has heard about it, and it makes me feel sort of jittery – good jittery – to think that I'm the one who brought it to life. That I helped to make more space in the world for people like me.

I haven't figured out what my favourite activity to do here is yet. I tried drawing, but I don't usually have enough time to finish whatever I get started on, and I find listening to music too stressful since I'm often overwhelmed by noise in school anyway. Being able to use the spare lockers in here is nice because it means that I can keep a selection of things that might be helpful to hand.

I look at the few things I've brought in so far and decide to take out my Belle keychain from Mum and the book Tom gave me for Christmas. I settle down on one of the floor cushions near the lamp and run my fingers over Tom's gift, still amazed that he picked it for me. It's a book of Eyvind Earle's illustrations, the man who painted the background art in *Sleeping Beauty*. Tom had called *Sleeping Beauty* boring when we watched it a few Christmases ago (and the story is a little), but the detail in the background paintings is remarkable. They took Earle six years to create and made *Sleeping Beauty* one of the most distinct Disney animated movies of all time. I find his illustrations soothing to look at, the shapes and the colours he uses.

I open the book to read over Tom's message on the inside.

Dear Freya, I don't often tell you you're great because, well, gross. But you are. Also, you were right – this movie is a work of art. Happy Christmas. From Tom.

It makes me smile every time I read it. I settle back against the wall and begin turning the pages, Belle resting on my lap. I have only a few minutes to savour this pocket of calm before the chaos of the school day begins, but a few minutes goes a long way in here. Besides, I know I can always come back later if I need to. That's the great thing about a space like this; no matter how overwhelmed or out of sorts I feel on a particular day, no matter how unpredictable things might get, in the back of my mind I know that there is somewhere quiet I can go to escape. Somewhere safe that helps me to feel calm and in control again. Somewhere I can be myself.

ACKNOWLEDGEMENTS

I would like to express my gratitude to the following people for their help in the writing and publishing of this book.

Firstly, to the late Michael O'Brien, for warmly welcoming me into The O'Brien Press family. It is an honour to be here. *Suaimhneas síoraí ort.* To my editor, Helen Carr, for her kindness, thoughtfulness, sensitivity and care. Thank you for taking Freya to your heart. To everyone at The O'Brien Press, for championing this book at every stage of its journey. It's been a privilege working with all of you.

To my creative writing cohort at Trinity, the first people ever to meet Freya. Thank you for your encouragement in those early days.

To my beta readers, Joyce O'Reilly, Jacq Murphy and Eve Geoghegan, for generously taking the time to read earlier drafts of the book and providing invaluable feedback.

To Mairéad Kiernan, my favourite person to earnestly discuss rom-coms and writing woes with. Thank you for your support and insight from day one.

Finally, to my husband, Stephen, for helping me unspool this story from my heart. It's been a while in the making; thank you for being there every step of the way.

AUTHOR'S NOTE

Thank you so much for choosing to read this book. If you enjoyed getting to know Freya, then I encourage you to seek out more autistic voices and continue deepening your understanding of the autistic experience. Below are some recommendations of books, films and documentaries I've enjoyed in recent years, all of which are either written by or centred on autistic people. I hope you enjoy them.

Loop on **Disney+:**

This heart-warming animated short film by Pixar SparkShorts tells the story of non-speaking Renee and her neurotypical peer, Marcus, who get stranded in a canoe at summer camp. They must find a way of communicating with and understanding each other to make their way back to shore. Featuring the voice of a non-speaking autistic actor and consulted on by autistic voices behind the scenes, this film is a wonderful example of inclusive filmmaking.

The Reason I Jump on **Disney+:**

Based on the book by Japanese autistic teenager, Naoki Higashida, this remarkable documentary follows the lives of a diverse group of non-speaking autistic people from around the world and offers a valuable insight into their rich inner lives. It showcases different cultural understandings of autism and demonstrates the transformative power of AAC (Augmentative and Alternative Communication), which enables non-speaking people to express themselves and communicate effectively with those around them. AAC can be unaided, like sign language or body language, and many non-speaking autistic people also use aided AAC, such as letterboards or smartphone/tablet communication apps.

Speechless by Fiacre Ryan:

The debut book by a young man from County Mayo, whom many people will recognise from the RTÉ documentary of the same name. Determined to prove his often-underestimated intelligence to the rest of the world, Fiacre decided to sit the Leaving Certificate in 2019, becoming the first non-verbal autistic person ever to do so in Ireland. This stunning collection of poetry and meditations on life is brimming with emotion, wit and intelligence, and demonstrates that, although a person might not speak, that doesn't mean they have nothing so say. It further demonstrates the important role families play in supporting and believing in the potential of their autistic loved ones.

This Is Not About Me **(available to rent on Apple iTunes, YouTube and Google Play Movies):**

Growing up, the emphasis in Jordyn Zimmerman's school reports related almost exclusively to behavioural challenges. Her educators lacked the understanding and resources to support her properly and she found school an immensely stressful environment as a result. When Jordyn finally encountered educators with the necessary patience, open-mindedness and skillset to teach her, she began to flourish. Through AAC, she could finally put language to her experience. She has since completed a Bachelor's degree in Education Policy and a Master's in Education, with a view to improving the education system for disabled students. This phenomenal documentary singlehandedly shatters every myth and misconception about the non-speaking autistic experience.

Diary of a Young Naturalist **by Dara McAnulty:**

Autistic people often have a great love for and feel a deep connection to the natural world, as is evident in the passionate work and activism of Greta Thunberg, Chris Packham and Dr Temple Grandin. These traits also shine though the beautiful, immersive writing of Dara McAnulty from Northern Ireland. A blogger, undergraduate student, and children's writer today, Dara's passion for wildlife and the environment stemmed from a fascination with the world around him when he was a small child. Dara writes about the natural world with sensitivity and spirit, and his close observations about the world around us make this book a feast for the senses.

What I Mean When I Say I'm Autistic: Unpuzzling A Life On the Autism Spectrum by Annie Kotowicz:

Part-memoir, part-manual, this enlightening book offers a refreshingly clear, concise and inclusive explanation of autism through the words of a woman identified as autistic in adulthood. Celebrating the unique joys and strengths of the autistic experience, as well as exploring and explaining the sensory, social and processing challenges many autistic people face, this short, thoughtfully written book has much to offer autistic people, their loved ones and anyone else curious to learn and understand more about neurodiversity and their fellow human beings.

Also available from

The O'Brien Press

FINDING A VOICE

KIM HOOD   FRIENDSHIP IS A TWO-WAY STREET ...

Shortlisted for the YA Book Prize

Jo can't tell anyone how hard it is living with her mentally ill mother. Chris literally has no way to speak at all. Together, can they finally find their voices?

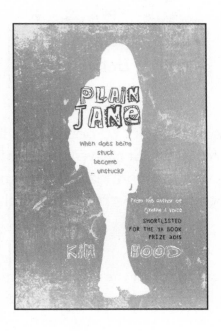

At nearly 16, Jane has lived in the shadow
of her little sister Emma's cancer diagnosis
for over three years. Nobody really cares
that her life is stuck in neutral; she is finding
it difficult to care herself ...